The Search for

Mrs. Claus

Courtney Daisey

Rescue House
Publishing

Courtney Daisey
The Search for Mrs. Claus

By

Courtney Daisey

* * * * *

Published by Rescue House Publishing

The Search for Mrs. Claus

Copyright 2014 by

Courtney Daisey

* * * * *

The Search for Mrs. Claus

publisher at requests@rescuehousepublishing.com. Thank you for

your support of the author's rights.

Editing: Jasmine Dawson

Formatting: Courtney Daisey and Nicholas Daisey

ISBN: 0692266240

ISBN-13: 978-0692266243

Courtney Daisey

* * * * *

This book is dedicated to my wonderful husband Nick.
Without him, none of this would have been possible. Also, this is
dedicated to my wonderful friend and beta reader Carolyn S. whose
help was often sought during the writing of this book.

* * * * *

The Search for Mrs. Claus

Courtney Daisey

__Chapter 1__

Snow was falling lightly on the icy ground. The trees were bare except for the thin icicles hanging from a few branches. His boots crunched the newly fallen snow as he strolled through the park. His weathered hands were tucked into the pockets of his light brown trench coat. He wore a dark red winter hat with flaps covering his frozen ears. His nose was red from the blasts of wind that whipped through the park and his cheeks were rosy. His white beard hid much of his face, but his bright blue eyes shone out as he watched the people passing by.

Beside him walked a much smaller man, one who could easily have been classified as a little person. The small man was skipping through the snow merrily just like the children they had seen playing in the park. He had a very long, thin beard and wore square, wire glasses. His head bore no hair and was covered in a bright green beret. The small man had a large grin on his face and spoke in a high, squeaky voice. "Isn't this fun, Nick? We don't get light, fluffy snow like this where we live!"

The older man, Nick, replied gently in a hushed voice, "Kringle, for the love of humanity please calm down. You aren't exactly blending in with the people here." Nick eyed the lime-green beret on Kringle's bald head. "We are in Quebec this year. At least can you pretend to be French Canadian?"

Kringle nodded. *"Oui oui, monsieur,"* he replied in his high squeaky voice. "But it does no good. The week is almost up and we still haven't found her."

The pair stopped beside a park bench near the pond. A thin layer of ice covered the pond and all of the ducks and geese had flown south for the winter. Nick sat down on the edge of the chilly bench and linked his fingers together. "I know. Sometimes I swear we'll never find her. We've been searching for over two hundred years now and never have any luck."

Kringle stopped skipping through the snow and hurried over to Nick. He patted the older man gently on the shoulder. "I know, but one day the prophecy will be fulfilled. We will find the perfect

8

wife for you and she will bring balance and harmony to the North

Pole forever. You can't give up."

Nick nodded. "I know I can't but it's so hard to find the

perfect woman in a week." He sighed gently. "Go on back up to the

workshop. I'll look around this evening and then I will come home.

It shouldn't be more than a couple of hours. Please let the other elves

know I didn't have any luck again this year. Perhaps next year will

be better. We haven't tried Europe in a while. Maybe Spain or

Belgium next year will yield a result."

Kringle wagged his finger at Nick. "Look here, as your Chief

Overseer of Elves I'm telling you now not to give up. Who knows?

Maybe you'll find her tonight before you come back. I'm waiting

until you get home before we say anything to the other elves. Now

stop sitting around and get back to looking!" The older elf wiggled

his nose and instantly disappeared with a pop that sounded like a

large bubble bursting.

Nicholas Claus had been searching for many years now

trying to find a woman who would fulfill the prophecy. When he'd

become Santa the elves told him of a prophecy that their leader would one day find a woman to bring home as his wife. This woman would be kind, friendly, and would be a helper to all at the North Pole. For one week out of the year at the end of November Nick was allowed to leave the North Pole and choose a city. He would spend the week in the city observing and trying to find a woman who would fit that persona. So far he'd had no luck at all. Sure he'd found kind, helpful friendly women but all were already married, which made them completely off limits. The younger ladies he'd found never had any interest in an old man so he'd continued his search the following year.

The laughter of a pair of young children brought him out of his reverie. He looked up to see a boy and a girl running through the park. The boy was running ahead and the little girl clutched a light brown teddy bear tightly to her chest as she ran behind him. Immediately he recognized them, as he knew all of the children in the world. The girl was having trouble keeping up with her brother. "Hey, wait up!" she called out as her brother ran across a long iron bridge over a narrow stream that fed into a small pond. The brother dashed past a young woman walking toward them. At that moment

10

the little girl's feet slipped on the icy bridge and she fell. The poor child landed on her behind and slid across the bridge, dropping the bear. The bear skidded across the bridge and fell into the stream. It landed in the icy water with a dull splash.

Immediately the little girl burst into tears. Nick stood and rushed towards the girl but the young woman stopped by her. He watched as she reached down and picked up the sobbing child and dried her tears. He couldn't make out her words, but the little girl nodded and pointed to the sopping wet teddy bear as it bobbed a few times and finally sank beneath the surface of the freezing stream. The woman was carrying several shopping bags and she reached into one and pulled out another teddy bear. The woman smiled and handed the little girl the bear. The child threw her arms around the woman's neck and held the bear tightly to her chest. The woman smiled, carried the little girl across the bridge, and gently lowered her to the ground. Her brother had stopped running and was standing there beside the bridge to help his little sister. The woman said something to the boy and he nodded as well. The he took his sister's hand and the pair walked away.

Nick crossed the bridge and stopped by the shopping bags the woman had set on the ground when she picked up the child. He picked up the bags and spoke gently to the woman. "That was very kind of you."

The woman turned to face him. She wore a red wool coat tied at her waist. Her long dark hair hung down her back and she had a matching red hat on her head. Around her neck she wore a white scarf. She held out her hands and Nick handed her the shopping bags. "Thanks. I felt so sad for the poor girl. Maybe now her brother will keep an eye on her a little better." Her voice was calm and soothing, much like that of a teacher.

"So few people would have done that for a stranger. You have a good heart, miss. May I ask your name?" Nick's voice was gentle as he spoke.

The woman smiled. "I'm Sophie. And you are?"

"I'm Nick," he replied and held out his hand.

Sophie reached out and accepted his outstretched hand. The moment their hands touched they felt a very strong jolt of electricity flow through them. They froze in place, their eyes locked on one another. The wind whipped around them but they remained still, gazing into each other's eyes. Finally Sophie broke the silence. "Nick…what are you doing later tonight?"

He smiled. "I didn't really have any plans. What do you have in mind?"

Breathlessly, Sophie released Nick's hand. "Well, I work at the Hotel Chateau Laurier. I'm a pastry chef by day and a lounge singer there by night. I'm performing tonight and if you'd like to come, I'd love to have you there."

He nodded and spoke softly. "I will see you then."

Sophie turned and headed back across the bridge. She stopped and looked over her shoulder. "The show starts at seven. I'll look for you." Then she turned and hurried away.

As Nick watched her go his heart was pounding. He'd shaken hands with thousands of women in his life and he'd never felt anything like that before. He stayed in that spot until Sophie was out of sight. Then he laid his finger aside his nose and nodded. He disappeared with a pop the same as Kringle had earlier.

Courtney Daisey

Chapter 2

Sophie hurried into the kitchen at the Hotel Chateau Laurier about ten minutes later. The kitchen was bustling with activity. The executive chef was hovering over one of the line cooks complaining about his knife skills and pointing to a pile of julienned carrots that were not uniformly sliced. The heavenly aroma of simmering marinara sauce wafted through the kitchen mingling with the harsher smell of the soap that eked out of the dish room. People were scurrying everywhere trying to finish preparations for the evening's meal. During her walk to work she hadn't been able to get the image of Nick's face out of her mind. There was something different about him, something special. She still hadn't calmed down and her face was flushed as she entered the kitchen. "Mira, are you here yet?"

"Yeah, I'm just dicing tomatoes for salads. What are you doing in here? You have to get ready for your performance tonight." Sophie's best friend Mira also worked at the hotel as a line cook.

Mira's hair was short, spiky, and light brown with streaks of purple throughout. She was petite and wore a pair of tight fitting

15

jeans under her chef's coat. Her pointy face was pale and devoid of make up. Her eyes were bright, almond shaped and dark brown. Her thin lips were smiling as she diced the tomatoes.

Sophie hurried over to Mira and dropped her shopping bags on the opposite counter. "You're never going to believe this, but I met this guy…"

"Wait!" Mira stopped dicing and faced her friend. "Never in the years we've known each other have you ever started a sentence that way. Sophia Marie Laurent never, ever meets guys!" Mira's dark eyes were twinkling with excitement. "So, spill it! Tell me everything!"

"Well, I met him in the park about ten minutes ago." Sophie leaned back against the counter and crossed her arms. "I seriously doubt it will go anywhere. I mean, this guy's clearly old enough to be my dad or grandfather. But he was just…different. And this was different in a good way."

Mira set her knife down and crossed her arms. "You met an older guy and he's got your heart racing like that? Wow, he must be pretty cool. So are you going to see him again?"

Sophie nodded. "Yeah. I invited him to the show tonight. We'll see if he comes."

Mira shrugged and turned back to her tomatoes. "Go get ready. If he comes, then we'll see what happens there. If not, there's nothing to worry about, right?"

Sophie picked up her shopping bags and headed off to the back to get ready. As the main act in the lounge she'd been given a very small dressing room. She entered the dressing room and dropped her bags on the small table in the corner of the room. Tonight was the first performance of the new Christmas themed show she would be performing. She looked through her costumes until she found the red dress she wanted to wear. The dress was long and form fitting. The satin material was donned with sparkling red sequins and flared slightly at the ankles. It didn't take her long to curl her hair and put on her make up. She shimmied into the long dress and glanced at the clock. She finished with ten minutes to spare. She slipped her feet into the red Jimmy Choo high heels that matched the dress and silently rolled her eyes thinking how much those shoes cost. Thankfully the hotel paid for all of her costumes. If it had been her choice she'd have bought a nice looking pair of red high heels from the discount shoe store across town but the hotel's general manager, Jeff, was insistent that she be dressed to impress on stage. She checked her makeup one final time in the mirror and headed out of her dressing room.

"Oh Sophie, that dress looks hot!" Mira grinned when she saw Sophie's performance outfit. "That's gonna knock every man in the room dead, as well as a few women!"

Sophie laughed. "Awesome! That's the plan. I really wasn't going to wear this one on the first night but I'm really hoping that Nick will show up."

Mira laughed. "Oh, if he doesn't he'll regret not seeing this! I bet some news reporter sees your show and plasters your photo on the front page!"

Mira headed back to the kitchen and Sophie wandered backstage until she reached the lounge. She peeked out through the curtains and scanned the crowd but didn't see Nick's face. She sighed. Maybe he wasn't going to come after all. *Oh well, it was too good to be true* she thought silently. The lights dimmed out front and she stepped onto the stage.

As the curtains rose she couldn't make out the faces of the people in the crowd. She'd have to get through her first song and let her eyes adjust. The piano began and she broke into an elegant, gentle rendition of *Silent Night*. As she sang she suddenly felt his eyes on her. She looked up and saw at the back of the crowd a tall man with a white beard enter the room. He wore a pair of khaki slacks and a crisp, white shirt with a burgundy blazer. He was taller than she, even in her Jimmy Choos. He came down the stairs and seated himself at a table near the front by the stage. Her eyes lit up when she saw him. He'd come to see her after all! She could see a sincere smile spread across his face as their eyes met. His snow-white hair and beard were neatly combed. His aquamarine eyes stayed locked on her as she sang.

As the song ended everyone broke into applause and she grinned at the crowd. She loved singing. It was such an integral part of her. When she sang she felt like she was baring her soul for all to see. It was a very personal act for her. As the crowd quieted down the band started playing and she began singing *Sing We Noel*. Her

eyes met Nick's as she sang and he was clearly spellbound by her.

She decided to be a little playful and use Nick as a bit of a

prop. She struck up a seductive rendition of *Santa Baby* and ended

up fawning over Nick throughout the whole song as if he were really

Santa. She circled his table, trailing her fingers over the back of his

chair as she glided behind it. When she came in front of the table she

leaned seductively over it, her eyes meeting Nick's. As he grinned

she winked at him. The crowd really got into it. By the time the song

was finished the crowd was roaring with applause and Nick's cheeks

were a bit pink.

The performance went beautifully and an hour later the show

was over. For an encore she did a hearty and fun version of *Santa*

Claus is Coming to Town but kept her eyes on Nick the whole time.

He did have the appearance of a good Santa Claus.

She went back to her dressing room to change and hung up

the sexy red dress. She put back on her black pants and white

sweater. Sophie donned her red hat and matching wool coat and put on her scarf. She gathered her shopping bags and headed for the kitchen.

The kitchen was bustling with activity so Mira stepped away from her line to chat with Sophie for a moment. "How did it go?"

"Fantastic! The crowd was really pleased with the performance." Sophie grinned. "And guess who showed up?"

Mira clapped her hands. "Oh really? What did he say?"

Sophie shrugged. "I haven't talked to him yet. I have a feeling he's going to be waiting outside for me though."

Mira nodded. "He probably will be out there. Look, go have fun but don't be taking any strange old men to bed tonight! I mean it!"

Sophie nodded in agreement. "Oh sex is the farthest thing from my mind right now, Mira. I promise you that."

As Sophie turned to leave Mira muttered, "It wasn't when you first got here. Girl, I could see it all over your face."

Sophie exited the back door of the kitchen and found herself in the alley behind the hotel. For an alley, the area was surprisingly well lit and she never worried about anyone mugging her. She

21

wrinkled her nose as she hurried past the row of reeking dumpsters along the brick wall and breathed in the fresh air as she reached the main street. Normally she turned left to head for home but tonight she turned right, just because she wanted to check and see if Nick was waiting out front for her. She walked slowly, looking for him. As she neared the main entrance to the hotel she smiled. He was there, hands in his pockets, standing a little ways away from the front of the hotel. "I wondered if you'd be here," she whispered as she neared him.

Nick laughed and smiled at her. "Oh yes, I wanted to tell you that I really enjoyed your performance."

"I'm so glad you did! When I took the stage I didn't see you but you came in soon after. Thank you for coming." Sophie sighed gently. She really wanted to get to know him more and wasn't ready to go home yet without learning more about him. "Look, I know this may be a bit presumptuous but would you like to go for coffee? There's a really great little coffee shop around the corner up here. It's quiet and we could talk, if you like."

Nick smiled at her. "I'd love that. Let's go. But I am going to carry your bags for you. It's the least I can do to help."

Sophie's heart fluttered in her chest as he reached out and took her shopping bags. She began walking and he walked beside her. "So, are you from Quebec, Nick?"

He shook his head. "No, I'm not from Quebec. I'm just in town...on business."

"Oh really? And what do you do for a living?" Sophie's curiosity was piqued.

Nick cleared his throat. "I...uh...am in the toy business. I work with a toy manufacturer."

Sophie giggled. "I swear, you are beginning to remind me of Santa Claus. The white beard and you make toys for a living? Yep, you really do sound a lot like Santa."

He winked at her. "What would you do if I told you I drove a sleigh with nine reindeer?"

"Nine? The stories say eight tiny reindeer." Sophie glanced over at him.

"Well, they weren't counting Rudolph when they wrote that story. You can't forget about him after all," he grinned.

Sophie couldn't help but laugh. He had such a great sense of humor. Her whole face lit up and she giggled at his words. But after all, Santa Claus wasn't real. She turned the conversation to something more realistic. "So, how long will you be in Quebec?"

Nick paused. "I'll be here as long as it takes me to accomplish my goal."

Sophie raised an eyebrow. "For your deal?"

He nodded. "Yes, once my deal is complete I'll be able to head home."

"And how long will that be?" Sophie's voice quivered.

The pair stopped outside the little coffee shop. Nick faced her, taking her hand in his. "That depends on the party with which I am dealing, Sophie. But let's not talk about my work right now. Right now I'd like to hear more about you."

She took a deep breath and led him into the coffee shop. Inside, the aroma of espresso and cappuccino permeated the air. The lights were low and there were several sofas lining the walls. A few

24

bistro tables were scattered throughout the room amongst cushy armchairs. There was a long counter on the right side of the room and a couple of baristas were working the machines there. Sophie stepped up to the counter and one of the baristas spoke to her. "Hey Sophie, what'll it be today?"

Sophie smiled. "I'll go with a large white chocolate mocha." She turned to Nick. "How about you?"

He cleared his throat. "I'll take a large hot chocolate please."

"Coming right up!" The barista turned to the machines and Sophie and Nick headed for one of the bistro tables. He held the chair for her as she sat and then seated himself across from her.

While they waited for their coffee the pair continued their conversation.

"So Sophie, are you from Quebec?" Nick asked softly.

She nodded. "Yes, I grew up here. I've lived in Quebec all of my life."

"Ah, I see. And you're a singer full time?" He listened as she spoke.

Sophie replied, "Part time actually. I'm a full time sous chef at the hotel. I love to cook. It's one of my three passions."

"Three? Most people only have one true passion. What are the other two?" Nick was quite curious as he waited for her reply.

"Cooking's one of them. Singing is second. And third is helping those less fortunate than me." Sophie sighed softly as she remembered the little girl in the park. "It's always good karma to pay it forward."

Nick cocked his head to one side. "Is that the only reason you pay it forward? For the good karma?"

Sophie shook her head. "Of course not. Even though I've had some…issues in the past I consider myself to be very fortunate. Not everyone in this world is as lucky and I have been. I want to help make the world a little bit brighter for those whose outlook is dim."

Nick smiled. "That's very positive, Sophie. I am glad you feel that way. I do as well."

The barista then brought their drinks over and Sophie took a sip of her coffee. "Oh, this is heaven! I tell you, this place always makes the best white chocolate mocha. It beats Starbucks and Caribou hands down."

Nick took a sip of his hot chocolate. It was rich, creamy, and very well flavored. "This is really good. It's some of the best hot chocolate I've had recently. I'll have to remember this place next time I'm in town."

"And how are often are you in town?" Sophie looked up from her coffee and her eyes met his.

"Once a year, usually for a very short time. But I may make plans to stop here more often." He smiled at her. "So tell me more about you. Do you have brothers and sisters?"

He noticed she immediately stiffened a bit and she shook her head. "No, I don't have any brothers or sisters." She cleared her throat. "I really don't know why I'm telling you this, but I have no family. You can imagine how tough the holidays are for me. So I do what I can to make sure that others have a good holiday season. I always work on Christmas so that the other chefs can have the day off with their families." She pointed to the shopping bags on the floor. "Look inside."

27

Nick leaned over and peered into a couple of the shopping bags. They were full of toys. "Toys?"

She nodded. "Yep, toys. I donate them to the homeless shelter each year so that the homeless children will have a good Christmas. It's my way of helping others. Throughout the year if I see toys on sale I'll buy them and save them up for Christmas. Then, on Christmas Eve I go to the shelter and give the toys to the workers there. They play Santa and distribute them to the children so they will have a good Christmas morning." She smiled forlornly. "If I can't have a good Christmas, I can at least make sure that others will. It's the least I can do. It's part of my good karma thing. This is my way of paying it forward."

Nick's heart ached for her. Here was this beautiful young woman with no family giving her all for others to make sure they had a good Christmas. Her selflessness warmed his heart. Part of him wanted to gather her in his arms, hold her, and tell her she'd be all right. But he knew that sort of physical contact was strictly off limits. Part of the prophecy was that his bride would be a virgin. If she really was the one meant for him, he'd have to keep that

28

boundary in place. That meant not putting either of them in a risqué situation. He'd only known her for a few hours and he already desired her but knew he had to let time run its course.

He reached out and covered her hand with his. "Sophie, you are a saint among women. You are the epitome of what Christmas really is about, giving to others to make them feel special. It's not about what you receive but about what you can give. And from what I can see, you give everything you have."

She smiled weakly and looked down at their hands. "I do what I can. I wish I could do more really. There are still so many children in the world who don't have a good Christmas. But I realize that I can't buy a toy for every child out there. I just do what I can and hope that it makes a difference for some.

Nick gently squeezed her hand. "You do, Sophie. You really do." He released her hand, picked up his hot chocolate, and downed it. "As much as it pains me to do this, I need to be going." He rose and looked down at her. "Can I see you again?"

Sophie nodded. "I was hoping you'd ask me that. Yes, I'd love to see you again. How about tomorrow evening? I don't have a show and will be off work at six. Why don't we meet outside of the hotel?"

He smiled gently. "I'm already looking forward to it. Until then, have a pleasant day." He turned and strolled out of the coffee shop.

Outside Kringle had appeared and ran over to Nick. "I've been watching you! You found her! You found her! You really really found her!"

Nick shushed the overly enigmatic elf. "Maybe. She's different from anyone I've ever met. I want to believe I've found her. She makes me feel different and special."

Kringle nodded. "I could see that! Don't think I haven't been watching you. That's what we elves do, you know. Make toys and keep an eye on others. Right now my eye is on you!" Kringle pointed a finger at his own eye and then at Nick. "Woo her, romance her, and make her fall for you but don't cross any lines mister! Got it?"

Nick softly sighed. "I know the prophecy, Kringle. And I just met the lady today! I'm not planning on crossing any lines. However

I am meeting her tomorrow night at six! I have no idea what we're going to do or where we're going to go but I'm looking forward to it. I really am looking forward to seeing her again."

Kringle grinned. "I bet you do and I know you want to see her again! But right now we have to get back to the North Pole! The elves are going to want to know why you're going to be absent during the busiest month of the year for us! It'll be worth it though. If this lady turns out to be the one, this will be worth it. Come on! Let's go!" Kringle wiggled his nose and disappeared with the sound of a popping bubble.

Nick looked back into the coffee shop window. Sophie was finishing her white chocolate mocha and getting up from her seat. He really wanted to walk her home but decided to play it by ear and wait until tomorrow to find out where she lived. He placed his finger aside his nose, nodded, and disappeared with a pop.

Courtney Daisey

Chapter 3

Sophie and Mira worked together preparing for a wedding banquet that weekend. Mira stirred a large bowl filled with a tuna for the bride's favorite appetizer, seared tuna bites. Sophie carefully molded pie crusts into tiny trays of a bite-sized tart pan. As she spooned the cherry mixture into the crust she inhaled the sweet scent of cherries and sugar and her stomach grumbled. She was lost in thought and didn't even hear Mira speaking to her. "Hello? Sophie? Snap out of it!"

Mira's increasingly loud voice brought Sophie out of her thoughts. "Oh, sorry. Did you say something?"

Mira sighed and turned to face her friend. "You've been lost in thought all day. What's on your mind? You usually aren't this quiet. Something's up."

Sophie set her whisk down and sighed. "I don't know, Mira. I'm usually so reserved, especially with guys. But last night we went for coffee and I ended up pouring my heart out to him. I told him about not having any family and about buying the presents for the homeless kids. Mira, I never do that! Why in the world did I open up to this guy like that? That's really not my style and you know it."

Mira shook her head. "I really don't know why you decided to open yourself to him, but somewhere deep inside I believe that you feel you can trust this guy. There's something about him that has brought your trust out. Girl, I know that's really rare for you." She looked at Sophie. "Are you going to see him again?"

"Yeah, tonight. He's coming by after work. We're meeting at six. I have no idea what we're going to do but I am definitely looking forward to it. There's something different about this guy. He makes me feel something I've never felt before. But he's old enough to be my grandfather! This is so weird." Sophie sighed and leaned back against the counter. "Is this okay? I mean I've got an interest in a guy who is old enough to have grandkids for Christ's sake. What if he does have grandkids? Could I become a grandmother at thirty-five? This isn't normal!"

Mira looked over at Sophie. "Forget about what's normal, Sophie. Emotions are never normal or cookie-cutter. For the first time in your life you've got feelings for a guy. Go with the flow on this one. See what happens. Who knows what will come of this. But if you aren't afraid to explore this emotion you may find that age is just a number."

"You really don't think I'm weird for having some sort of instant connection with an old guy?" Sophie's eyes widened a bit as she looked at her friend.

Mira shook her head. "Honey, who you decide you love has nothing to do with age. Sure there are people who may judge you for dating an older man but don't worry about that. What's important is that you both are happy. Right now you've just met so feel this out. Explore your feelings for the guy. See where it goes. Only you can decide if this is right for you or not. So go with it. Enjoy it. And if he's the one for you, you'll know it."

Sophie sighed. "He better not be another Jeff though. I'm not going to tolerate that."

Mira nodded. "Nor should you! I mean, when Jeff asked you out that time I thought that maybe something good would be coming your way. He is cute, after all."

"Yeah, he's cute all right." Sophie's brow furrowed. "Cute and conceited and thinks he's God's gift to women. We went for coffee and he was all over me! Jeff didn't understand the meaning of the word *no* at all. He tried to grab me and I just felt so…icky, for lack of a better word. I told him I wanted to get to know someone before taking things to a physical level and the next thing I knew he was spreading stories about my lack of experience to all of the guys around! Remember how he kept saying that I couldn't handle a real man? Well, I learned quickly that he wasn't a real man at all." She rolled her eyes. "Then he got promoted and I just wanted to crawl under a rock! I still can't believe we work for that jerk now."

Mira nodded in agreement. "No kidding! I wonder who he slept with to get the job? Well at least he hasn't bothered you since then."

"He knows better, or he'll be looking for a new job in a different hotel." Sophie winked. "Men just need to learn how to respect women. So few do now. If I ever date again, my man will be kind and respectful toward women."

Mira grinned. "I bet Nick is! He seemed like such a

gentleman from what you've told me."

"He really is!" Sophie thought back to the previous night and

smiled softly. "He's different and I like different."

"Good! You're different too and I bet he likes that as well."

Mire smiled warmly at her friend.

Sophie hugged Mira. "Thanks. I feel better now. You have

that effect on people, really."

Mira laughed. "Anytime! Now get your bite sized cherry tarts

finished and go on your date."

A few minutes before six Sophie had finished with her tarts,

changed clothes, and stepped outside. She came out of the alley onto

the main road and saw Nick standing there in front of the hotel, just

as she'd seen him the previous night. She strolled up to him. "We're

going to have to stop meeting like this." She giggled at her own joke

and smiled at him. "It's good to see you."

Nick smiled back at her and reached for her hand. "It's a

pleasure to see you too, Sophie. I have something planned for us this evening. I figured we could get to know each other more. Please come with me."

Sophie allowed Nick to link his fingers with hers. It was a magical feeling. That electricity jolted through both of them as their fingers linked. They walked in silence, both lost in the physical connection of their hands. Nick led her through the park and on the other side there was a carriage with two white horses. "If you like, we can take a carriage ride together and talk more."

She smiled. "I'd love to!"

Nick paid the carriage driver and helped Sophie into the carriage. She sat down and he climbed in beside her. He spread a blanket over both of their legs to keep them warm. The carriage driver clucked to the horses and slowly they moved forward.

The carriage was made of white oak and was polished so that the wood shone in the moonlight. The seats were comfy and covered with purple velveteen. The driver wore a top hat and a thick coat over his suit. The two horses that pulled the carriage were both white and had long, flowing manes and tails.

The Search for Mrs. Claus

Sophie had never been on a carriage ride before. She could hear the sounds of the city outside the park and yet she was at peace. The wind blew lightly through the icicle-covered trees causing them to make a light tinkling sound as they clinked together. She could hear the clip clop sound of the horses' hooves as they walked forward. They rode in silence for a while listening to the sounds around them. Finally Nick spoke.

"Sophie, last night you'd mentioned that you have no family." She tensed up at his words. Nick reached over and took both of her hands in his and looked deeply into her eyes. "Please tell me what happened. How did you come to be alone? I know this is a tough subject for you, but I care and would like to know what happened."

She sighed gently as her eyes stayed locked with his. There was something about looking into his eyes that made her feel safe and relaxed. She barely knew the man but she could tell that he was sincere and that she could trust him. She decided to tell him her story. Sophie took a deep breath and began.

Courtney Daisey

"I was born to Jacques and Anna Laurent thirty five years ago. He was from Quebec and she had come from France to visit family who lived here. They met at a party her family was hosting. They really hit it off right away and even after she returned to France they wrote letters to one another. Finally my dad took a trip to France to see her again and he ended up proposing to her while he was there. It was very sudden, much like a typical romance novel. She moved back to Quebec with him, learned English, and became a teacher. My dad was a chef and once I was born he began to teach me all about cooking. They never had any other children, though it wasn't for a lack of trying. See, both of them also had no brothers or sisters so they wanted a large family. It just didn't happen for them though. As I got older my dad could tell that I had acquired some skill in the kitchen and he taught me everything he could. After I graduated from high school I enrolled in culinary school in New York and I moved to America."

Sophie paused and her face darkened. "My parents were coming to see me during the Christmas holidays and their rental car hit a patch of black ice. They spun into oncoming traffic and were hit head on by a tractor-trailer. They both died instantly, or that's what

the police told me. After I finished culinary school I came back to

Quebec, rented a small apartment, and found a job as a pastry chef at

the Hotel Chateau Laurier. I've been there ever since. And each

Christmas, which is a very difficult holiday for me, I donate my time

and money to buy toys for the less fortunate. I also volunteer to work

most major holidays at the hotel so that those who do have families

can be off and be with their loved ones."

She paused once more and looked over at Nick. "I've never

had a boyfriend, never been kissed, and never been on a real date.

Tonight's my first date…if we are calling it that. These feelings and

emotions inside me are completely new and I really don't know what

to make of this." Her eyes met his. "I just know that I've never felt

this way before about anyone."

Nick smiled at her and gently squeezed her hands. "Sophie, I

also have never had a girlfriend, never been kissed, and never have

been on a first date…until tonight. You are my first date. I'm hoping

the other two will come, but I am terrified to rush into things. So let's take our time and see where this goes. I'm game if you are." His

eyes twinkled playfully as he spoke his last sentence.

Sophie grinned. "Me too." She leaned back against the seat

and hesitantly leaned to the right, pressing her shoulder against his.

He slipped his arms around her and pulled her close to his side. Her

heart pounded as she snuggled against him and rested her head on

his shoulder. *So this is what love feels like,* she thought inwardly.

She quickly decided she liked this new feeling. It was different and

very special.

As they rode along she turned her head toward him and

spoke quietly. "So, I've told you about my life. It's your turn. Tell

me all about you."

Nick froze. He knew he couldn't tell her everything, as that

would give his secret away. But he could divulge some facts about

himself, particularly the information from before he became Santa

Claus. He cleared his throat. "Well, I was born in France, in a small

village north of Paris. My mother stayed home and my father…he

was a carpenter. He built houses for a living. I also didn't have any

brothers or sisters. It was just me. As I grew I began to work with my father, much like you did. He began to teach me the art of carpentry. As it turns out, I had more of a knack for whittling and making smaller things. I began to make some toys by hand." He paused, thinking about how much he could say. Finally he continued. "Eventually I joined a toy company and was able to teach other people how to make toys in the method I'd used. As the years have gone by the systems have become automated and much less is done by hand. But the end product is still the same. The children of the world are still happy to receive them."

Sophie smiled up at him. "I swear you sound more and more like Santa Claus every day. You probably hear that a lot though."

"I do, but I don't object to that. After all, who doesn't like Santa Claus?" He winked at her.

The carriage stopped and had returned to their point of origin. Nick folded up the blanket that covered their laps and placed it back on the opposite seat. He exited the carriage and helped Sophie down.

"Sophie, may I walk you home?" Nick asked, his twinkling blue eyes meeting hers.

43

She nodded. "I'd like that." She slipped her hand into the crook of his elbow and the pair began walking. "Nick, it was really liberating to tell you about my past. It's like a weight has been lifted off my shoulders. Thank you, really, for letting me do that."

"You're more than welcome, my dear." Nick's voice was gentle and calm as he spoke.

Her heart leapt in her chest at the term of endearment. No one had ever called her that before and she felt elated.

The walk back to Sophie's apartment was short and soon the pair found themselves standing outside of Sophie's door. She lived on the second floor of a loft-style apartment complex. "Nick, I'd like to thank you for an absolutely wonderful evening." She took his hands in hers. "When can I see you again?"

Nick squeezed her hands gently. "How about tomorrow night?"

She sighed. "I'm performing tomorrow night. Why don't you come to the show and we'll get some dinner afterward?"

He smiled. "I'd like that."

The pair grew silent as they looked into one another's eyes. Their hands remained linked and both were waiting to see what the other would do. Finally, Nick leaned forward and placed a very light kiss on her cheek. "I'll see you tomorrow." He released her hands and turned to head down the stairs.

Sophie unlocked her front door and wandered into her apartment. Did this classify as a first kiss? Since her lips didn't touch his, she decided that it did not, but it was really close. She reached up and lightly touched her cheek where his lips had brushed her skin. Her heart was still pounding in her chest.

Hoping to catch a glimpse of him walking she hurried to her window and looked down at the front door. She watched for ten minutes but to her dismay he never exited the building. Where he went, she did not know, but he wasn't walking down the street. *Now where in the world did he go?*

<u>Chapter 4</u>

The next day at work Sophie couldn't stop talking about the previous night. Mira listened as Sophie rattled on about the carriage ride, spilling her entire family history to him, and letting him walk her home. Her whole face lit up when she told Mira about the kiss on her cheek. "Oh I really was hoping he'd kiss me…you know…on the lips, but he didn't. I guess because he's just as inexperienced as I am and wanted to take it slow. What do you think about it?"

Mira laughed. "I think you're over-thinking this kiss, Sophie. Yes, he's as inexperienced as you are but he probably wasn't sure how you'd react. Tonight, when you two go out, if you want to kiss him just do it! Take the lead, girl! Grab the bull by the horns, so to speak."

Sophie's eyes widened. "Oh Lord, I can't do that! Isn't it the man's job to take the lead on physical things in a relationship?"

Mira burst into laughter. "Sure, fifty years ago! It's the twenty-first century! It's perfectly all right for the woman to take the lead in this day. Go for it if you want it!"

Sophie turned back to the cake she was icing. "Oh believe me, I want it. I've never felt like this before. But what if I scare him off by letting him know I'd like to go further?"

"Look, we're not talking about hopping into bed with him right now, Sophie! We're just talking about kissing. If you want to kiss the man, just do it. We'll deal with the rest of it later. But tonight if you want to experience that kiss, just lean in, and go for it." Mira's voice was firm but kind.

"Okay, we'll see what happens. After the show tonight we're going out for dinner. Where should we go? I'm the one who invited him so I have to pick the place. Should we go somewhere romantic or somewhere laid back? Where do I take a guy for a date? Oh, this is so hard!" Sophie wrung her hands, desperation resounding in her nervous tone.

Mira giggled. "It depends on what you're both in the mood for. Find out after the show. Don't think too hard about it. Really, just go with the flow. If you want Chinese, go for it. If you want steak, go for that. Just make up your mind tonight. Live in the moment and don't try to plan everything out. It'll be more fun that way."

"I don't have to plan everything out? I thought part of dating was having outings planned ahead of time." Sophie cocked her head to one side.

Mira shook her head. "Oh no, that's not how it works at all. See, there are times that you may want to plan out a special evening. But most of the time dating is spontaneous. It's a spur-of-the-moment sort of thing. If you want to go see a movie, go for it. If you want to go to dinner, enjoy yourselves! If you want to just sit on the couch, watch a movie, and eat popcorn, that's part of dating too. You don't have to plan an evening out or go somewhere expensive to be on a date. Honestly, you should take an evening and prepare dinner for him at your place. And afterwards turn on the DVD player and watch a movie together. See, that way if you're in the mood to get a little more physical you're in a private place and not in some movie theater." Mira winked at her. "Trust me, that happens a lot."

Sophie's eyes widened again. "Oh Mira! I never knew you were such a wild child!"

Mira exploded into laughter. "Oh, you have no idea of the various places I've gotten frisky with a guy! Once you get more experience we can swap stories! But for now, don't stress about that. Just have fun."

After her shift in the kitchen was done Sophie retreated to her dressing room to prepare for the show. She rifled through her costumes and opted for a low cut sleeveless white ball gown with a sequined bodice and a long, flowing satin skirt. She slipped her feet into a pair of white high heels and pulled her hair back into an elegant bun. She applied her makeup thoughtfully tonight. After all, Nick would be there to watch her. After putting on a pair of diamond earrings and a matching necklace she was ready. She stepped out of her dressing room and approached the stage. The curtains were still drawn and she peeked through. Sure enough, Nick was seated at a table by the stage. He kept looking over at the pair of rowdy, boisterous businessmen at the table to the left of him. One of them wore a tall, gray Stetson and seemed to be on his third or fourth drink. His words were slurring already. Sophie rolled her eyes. Hopefully the half drunk guys would behave throughout the show.

She stepped back as the curtains rose and the pianist began playing. Her gentle voice began singing the sweet melody of *Silent Night* and the crowd went silent as she sang. Nick was spellbound as he watched her. Sophie's voice was clear and pure as she sang about the birth of Christ and his heart swelled with affection.

As the song ended the pair of rowdy businessmen applauded louder than anyone. The one in the gray Stetson jumped to his feet, clapping raucously. "Sing one for me, baby doll!" he hollered above the crowd.

Sophie was very professional and ignored the loud, obnoxious man. She went into her second number and began walking the stage, making eye contact with various members of the crowd and smiling at them to connect with them. She glanced over at the man in the gray Stetson. His eyes looked her up and down and he licked his lips. She shivered and looked elsewhere, trying to put him out of her mind. Once again as the song ended the man in the Stetson was louder than the rest of the applauding crowd. "Come on over and sing one just for me, sugar," he yelled at Sophie.

As she went into the third song of the set she walked close to the edge of the stage and the man in the Stetson stood up and grabbed her hand. "Come down here and sing that one just for me, honey," he said and pulled Sophie off the stage and into his lap.

Before the security detail even had a chance to get to Sophie Nick leaped out of his seat, wrenched the man's hand from Sophie's wrist, and pulled her out of the inebriated man's lap. "Sir, this is a classy act and not some burlesque show. I advise you to leave now," Nick growled, his voice dark. He pulled Sophie behind him, putting himself between her and the drunken man. His eyes narrowed as he stared the man in the Stetson down.

At that moment the security detail arrived and hauled the man out of the lounge. Nick turned to Sophie who was shaking. "Are you all right?"

Sophie nodded, unable to speak for a moment. No one had ever done that in one of her shows before. Either this man was completely drunk or completely stupid...or maybe both. "I'm fine," she squeaked, her voice quivering with fright.

The hotel's general manager, Jeff, suddenly took the stage. "Ladies and gentlemen, I sincerely apologize but for the safety of my singer the remainder of tonight's show has been cancelled. Your tickets will be refunded and I hope you will come another night for the performance." He hopped off the stage and rushed over to Sophie. "Are you all right? What happened?"

Before Sophie could speak Nick said, "She was accosted by some guest who has consumed far too much whiskey for his own good. Thankfully he's been removed from the premises but Sophie isn't herself right now."

Jeff looked at Nick and the back to Sophie. "Do you know this man?"

Sophie nodded and managed to speak, her voice still shaky. "Yes, this is my boyfriend, Nick. I'm so grateful he was here. He got to me before security did, thankfully."

Jeff looked at Nick quizzically and then sighed. "All right then. Take the rest of the night off. Take tomorrow too. The kitchen will manage. Just get some rest. We'll see you in a couple of days."

Sophie nodded in agreement and he left her alone with Nick. The majority of the crowd had dissipated. "I need to go change."

Nick nodded. "Yes, you really can't be wearing that home. However, may I at least tell you that you look beautiful?"

Sophie's cheeks tinged pink at his words. No man had ever called her beautiful before. "Thank you," she mumbled, uncertain what to say.

He helped Sophie back up onto the stage and guided her backstage. "I'll wait outside your dressing room while you get changed."

Sophie opened her dressing room door and went inside, closing the door behind her. It was then that she was overwhelmed with the emotion of what had just taken place. She collapsed onto the floor and dissolved into tears. Her entire body shook as she sobbed. Moments later her door flung open and Mira came barreling into the room. "What the hell happened Sophie? Jeff told me to come and check on you."

Mira dropped to her knees and gathered Sophie in her arms. Between sobs Sophie managed to squeak out a few words. "Stupid guy…big hat…pulled me off the stage…"

"Oh crap, are you hurt?" Mira looked her friend over.

Sophie shook her head and tried to wipe the flowing tears from her cheeks. "No, I'm not hurt. Nick…he pulled the guy off me."

Now it was Mira's turn to be surprised. "He did? Wow, how'd he do that?"

Sophie wiped her face off with the back of her hand. "He's stronger than he looks. I'm really glad he was there. Jeff cancelled the rest of the show and told me to take all of tomorrow off."

"Wow, what a night! Jeff never gives people random nights off." Mira stood up and pulled Sophie to her feet. "Look, we've got to get you changed and safely back home. Nick's waiting outside for you."

Sophie's eyes widened. "Oh good Lord! I told Jeff that Nick was my boyfriend. The whole hotel's going to know Sophia Marie Laurent is finally in a relationship now."

Mira smiled gently. "Oh that's no problem. Yeah, we all know Jeff's a chatterbox and will announce your news to the world but that's okay."

"But, what if Nick wasn't ready to announce that to the world? What if he wanted to keep it secret for a while?" Sophie stepped out of the Jimmy Choos and nudged them across the floor with her bare feet toward the wall.

"Well, it's too late now." Mira smiled and helped Sophie get her ball gown off and passed her regular clothes to her. She hung up the gown while Sophie dressed. "Besides, I don't think Nick will mind. After all, he came to your rescue like a knight on a white horse tonight. Girl, he's got it for you, big time."

Sophie slipped her feet back into her work shoes. "He's not the only one. I'm nuts about the guy."

Mira helped Sophie into her red wool coat and the pair exited the dressing room. Standing outside were general manager Jeff and Nick. The guys appeared to have been deep in conversation. The both hushed when the ladies emerged. "Sophie, are you sure you're all right?" Jeff asked.

Sophie nodded. "Yeah, I'm fine. I just need a good night's rest to clear my head."

Jeff nodded in agreement. "That you do. Go on home. Nick's assured me that he'll keep an eye on you tonight. We'll see you in a couple of days."

"All right. Thanks Jeff." Sophie spoke softly and looked up at Nick. The worry he felt was clearly evident in his eyes. "Let's go."

Mira and Jeff left the pair alone and Nick walked Sophie out. He kept his arm around her waist and having it there made Sophie feel at ease. He was there and nothing would happen to her as long as he was there. But after he left for the evening, would she still feel all right?

The pair walked in silence to Sophie's apartment. They ascended the stairs together and Sophie unlocked the door. "Nick, please do come in. I'm so sorry that our plans for the evening have been ruined. Maybe we can order a pizza and watch a movie here?"

Nick smiled. "I'd love that. What do you like on your pizza?"

"Pepperoni with extra sauce," Sophie replied.

"That sounds perfect," Nick said gently. "I love extra sauce."

The pair entered Sophie's apartment and she flipped on the light. It was a small apartment with two bedrooms, a tiny kitchen, and an open living room. The concrete floors of the loft apartment were covered in various rugs. An old brown couch was against the right wall and the television sat on a dresser opposite the couch. The end tables didn't match and neither did the lamps on the tables. The kitchen was clean and tidy, just as Nick imagined a chef's personal kitchen would be. There was a small round wooden table in the corner of the kitchen with two chairs.

She took off her coat and hung it over one of the chairs. Nick did the same with his coat as well.

Sophie picked up the cordless phone and dialed the local pizza place. She ordered the large pizza with pepperoni and extra sauce. After hanging up the phone she turned to Nick. "Please, make yourself at home. What kind of movies are you into? Action? Romance? Documentaries? I've got a variety of movies. Just take a look in the cabinet under the TV and pick something. The pizza should be here in about fifteen minutes."

"Your pizza place must be really close then." Nick opened

the cabinet and began rifling through the movies.

"Yep, it's next door. They know me well." Sophie opened

the fridge and pulled out a two-liter bottle of Coke. "You like

Coke?"

Nick nodded. "Yes, that will be just fine." He pulled a movie

out of the cabinet and closed the doors.

"What did you pick?" Sophie asked as she opened the bottle

and poured two glasses of Coke.

"I hope you don't mind, but I decided on *The Sound of*

Music. Your voice rivals that of the great Julie Andrews and I've

always loved this movie." He handed her the DVD and smiled at her.

Sophie blushed and opened the plastic case. "I love Julie

Andrews. She's got an amazing voice. When I was a kid I grew up

on this movie and on her singing. She was my inspiration. For you to

compliment me in such a way absolutely makes my day. Thank

you." She popped the DVD into the player and pressed a few

buttons.

Nick sat down on the couch and Sophie brought their glasses of Coke in to the living room. She set them down on the coffee table and kicked her shoes off. "Oh, I hope you don't mind but I'm pretty informal around here. After all, it's just me."

Nick smiled and slipped his shoes off as well. "I like being informal. It's much more fun and real."

The doorbell rang and Nick reached into his pocket. Sophie noticed this. "What are you doing?" She watched him as he dug around in his pocket.

"Paying for dinner," he replied. He pulled out some money. "We may not be actually going out, but it's a gentleman's job to take care of the lady's dinner after all."

Sophie's cheeks turned pink as his kind words. "That was unexpected. Thank you," she whispered and allowed Nick to head for the door. He opened the door, paid the delivery guy, and returned to the couch with the pizza box. Sophie sank into the old, soft couch and Nick placed the cardboard box on the coffee table.

She opened the box and inhaled the aroma of the melted mozzarella, sweet marinara sauce, and the mouth-watering pepperoni. "Pizza, Coke, and Julie Andrews. This night can't get any better!"

Nick looked at her and spoke softly. "All of those plus the company of one lovely woman…yep, this evening's perfect."

Sophie blushed as she pressed the play button on the remote to start the movie. She really had no witty comeback for his comment so she simply replied, "Thank you, Nick."

Three hours later as the Von Trappe family was crossing the mountain range into Switzerland most of the pizza was gone, and Sophie was snuggled against Nick as she drifted in and out of sleep. He picked up the remote and turned off the TV. The sound of the TV turning off roused Sophie and she looked up at Nick. "Oh, the movie's over?"

He nodded and spoke softly. "Yes, it is. It's late and you should get some rest."

Sophie turned to face him. Their faces were inches apart. She remembered Mira's words. *Just go for it.* She closed her eyes and slowly leaned toward him. Moments later their lips met gently.

The sensation shot desire through her body like wildfire. She didn't know what to think as their lips moved against one another. All she could think about was him. She slid her arms around him and he pulled her tightly against him, deepening the kiss. Slowly her lips parted and he thrust his tongue gently inside her waiting mouth. She gasped at the entry but liked it immediately. She moaned and pressed her body against his. She couldn't get enough of this new feeling.

His arms tightened around her, holding her close. Slowly his fingertips began tracing lightly up and down her back. She shivered in delight at the sensation as their tongues warred. Slowly, Nick pulled back. Sophie whimpered in protest as the kiss broke and they sat looking into each another's eyes.

"Stay with me," Sophie asked breathlessly.

Nick shook his head. "I can't. Not tonight." He cupped her face in his hands and looked deeply into her eyes. "Believe me, it's not for lack of desire. I want to so badly. But if I do, we may both do something we'll both regret. We've only just met. We have to take it slowly. Sophie, I desire you and want to experience more with you but we have to take our time. Promise me we can see each other tomorrow though."

Sophie breathed deeply, trying to come back to earth from the proverbial cloud she'd been riding. "Definitely. Come by anytime. I'll be here."

Nick smiled and leaned down to gently kiss her once more. Even that light touch of his lips on hers set her body on fire again. "Good night, beautiful lady."

Nick stood up and headed for the kitchen to retrieve his coat. He let himself out as Sophie watched him go, her head still spinning.

She didn't even realize he'd left until she heard the door close. She jumped up and darted to the door. She flung it open to tell him good-bye but he was gone. She ran down the stairs to catch him before he went outside but he was nowhere to be seen. She opened the door to the building but she didn't even see his footprints in the newly fallen snow. He'd simply vanished.

Chapter 5

Nick reappeared in his living room at the North Pole. Kringle was there looking into a scrying bowl and looked up at Nick with disapproval. "Tsk tsk, Mr. Claus," Kringle's singsong voice rang out loudly. "No hanky panky without a ringy on her fingey!"

Nick rolled his eyes. "Oh shush, Kringle. Since you were watching me so closely you'll know that I left before something could happen."

Kringle waved his hand in the air to dismiss Nick's words. "Oh whatever. That was one heck of a passionate kiss! That really could have gone somewhere!"

"I wanted it to." Nick sat down in his cushy green armchair across from Kringle. "God knows I wanted to take that further. She did too. After all, she asked me to stay with her." Nick ran his hands through his long, wavy, snow-white hair. "It was so hard to say no, Kringle. I've never wanted anything more than I want her."

Kringle clapped his hands. "So you do have it in you! Desire's one step of this process! But now it's got to go further. This has to be more than just the physical wanting of the woman. This has to be a meeting of the hearts as well."

"But Kringle, it is. There's something about her that makes me feel things I've never felt before." Nick sighed, remembering the feel of Sophie in his arms, her lips pressed against his. He turned back to the old elf. "Were you watching all night long? Did you see what happened at her show?"

Kringle nodded. "Yeah, I did. That nasty man pulled her off the stage. But you were there to rescue her."

"It's a real good thing for him that my magic doesn't allow me to do any harm. Otherwise he'd be in a world of pain right now," Nick growled as he recalled the incident, his hands balling into fists in anger. "I really wanted to deck the guy. He deserved it."

"Calm down, Prince Charming. You rescued the girl. But in order to live happily ever after you need to keep your hormones in check." Kringle hopped up into the coffee table and glared at Nick. "I know you want her but if the prophecy is going to be fulfilled she has to remain pure. Don't screw this up…literally!"

Nick laughed. "Good one, Kringle. I promise to keep my hormones in check. You have to promise something too though."

"Oh really? What's that?" Kringle asked curiously.

Nick looked Kringle right in the eye. "Stay out of my house on my wedding night!"

Kringle roared with laughter. He fell off the coffee table, grabbed his belly, and rolled on the floor as he laughed. When he finally caught his breath he replied, "You don't have to worry about that! I'll be far away from earshot of this place!"

Back at Sophie's apartment she was on the phone with Mira talking about the exact same subject.

"And then, he just left. He says he wants to take things slow but I am terrified that I did something wrong. What if I was a terrible kisser? Maybe I should research kissing online and see what I need to do to make myself better at this…" Sophie rattled on.

"Stop!" Mira interrupted. "His leaving had absolutely nothing to do with your…techniques. He's an older gentleman from a different generation. True gentlemen aren't apt to just hop in the sack with a woman right away. He wants to do the honorable thing and get to know you on a personal level first. There's absolutely

nothing wrong with that. Honestly, that's rare in today's world."

Sophie flopped down on the couch where she'd been

cuddling with Nick earlier. "Are you sure?"

Mira replied, "Absolutely. Look, he'll be back tomorrow to

see you. Both of you are going to have the kiss on your minds so

break the ice. When he walks in the door kiss him right then and

there. That will get the ice broken. Then you'll be able to do other

things without worrying about what the other is thinking regarding

the kiss."

Sophie sighed. "God, I still can't believe I asked him to stay!

I've never asked a guy that before."

"Well, there's a first time for everything!" Mira replied.

Sophie sighed. "Apparently tonight's not that night though.

All right, we'll see what happens." She hung up the phone and

leaned back into the cushions of her old brown couch. Not long ago

she was involved in a deep passionate kiss right in this very spot.

She only hoped that Nick was thinking about it as much as she was.

She pulled a throw blanket over her and fell asleep in the spot where she and Nick had both shared their first kiss.

The next morning Sophie awoke and headed for her shower. She had never fallen asleep on her couch and stayed there all night before. She reached her bathroom and stripped her clothes off. She turned on the water and stepped into the hot shower. The water cascaded over her body and she leaned her head back under the spray. Even there her thoughts drifted back to Nick. Oh, how she wanted to kiss him again! She washed her body and hair, rinsed off, and stepped out of the shower.

Sophie wrapped her hair up in a towel and padded out of the bathroom and into her bedroom. She rifled through her dresser until she came up with a pair of sweat pants and an old comfy sweater. As she was drying her hair with the towel, her doorbell rang. She walked to the door and opened it. There stood Nick who looked delighted to see her.

Her heart skipped a beat when she saw him. Immediately she remembered his lips on hers and how it felt to be in his arms. She recalled Mira's advice. *When he walks in the door, kiss him right then and there.* She stepped into the hallway, wrapped her arms around him, and planted her lips on his. She smiled inside when his arms engulfed her and his hands caressed her back. Hesitantly, she opened her mouth and he thrust his tongue inside. Instantly, her body was set on fire. She melted against him into the passionate kiss. Then she remembered she needed to be the one to end the kiss this time. Reluctantly, she stepped back. "I wasn't expecting you yet, but thanks for coming," she said breathlessly.

Nick smiled. "I honestly wasn't expecting to come by this early but the truth is I couldn't stop thinking about you all night." He reached out and gently caressed her cheek with his hand. "I hope you don't mind me stopping by so early."

"Oh, not at all. I'm really glad you did. Come on in." Sophie stepped back and let Nick enter the apartment. "Let me go finish with my hair and I'll be right back." She headed back into the bathroom and Nick sat down on the couch.

He couldn't get the feel of that second kiss out of his thoughts. He remembered the scent of her shampoo and the feel of her arms around him. His heart pounded in his chest. God how he wanted more! But he knew Kringle was watching and would already give him grief about this second passionate kiss. He'd never felt physical desire before and controlling it was extremely hard.

Sophie returned a few minutes later with her wet hair brushed out and pulled back into a loose ponytail at the nape of her neck. She flopped down on the couch beside him. "So, what do you have in mind for today? Do you want to go somewhere or just have a lazy, relaxing day here?"

Nick took her hand in his. The thought of spending a lazy day curled up on the sofa with this entrancing woman in his arms was extremely tempting. Nick knew where temptation would lead though. He cleared his throat, brushing that thought from his mind. "I have something I'd like to show you. It's a present."

"A present? Wow, thank you! But I didn't do anything to deserve a present yet." Sophie smiled gently at him.

"That's the point. It's a just-because-I-wanted-to present. But it's not here. We have to go out to get it." Nick's bright eyes twinkled with excitement. "So come on. Do you need to dry your hair first? After all we are going outside."

Sophie shook her head. "Oh no, I'll be just fine. Let me grab some shoes." As she stood and got off the couch Nick shook his head and pointed a finger at her back wiggling it slightly. Instantly her hair was dry. Sophie reached up and felt her suddenly dry hair. A confused look appeared on her face and she turned to face him. "Wow, that's never happened before! My hair's dry!"

Nick nodded. "I see. Maybe you walked under a warm air vent or something. But don't worry about that. Do you want to go?"

Sophie nodded. "Yep, be right back."

Nick put his coat back on and picked up hers. He probably shouldn't have dried her hair, but he didn't want to risk her getting pneumonia by going out in the icy temperature with wet hair. Momentarily, she returned with her shoes on. He helped her into her coat and they headed outside. Once on the front steps Nick took her hand. "Come with me."

The pair walked in silence down the busy street. Cars drove by quickly, tossing slush from their tires onto the sidewalks and into other lanes. The sidewalks were crawling with people hurrying to work, appointments, or other places. Fortunately the wind was

calmer today but it was still bitterly cold outside.

Nick led Sophie several blocks down and turned onto another

street. She recognized the street immediately. "Nick, why are you

taking me to work? I'm off today."

He winked at her. "Patience is a virtue, Sophie. You'll see

shortly."

She grinned. "Patience may be a virtue, but it's one I don't

have. I'm dying to know what your surprise is!"

He laughed as he led her into the lobby of the hotel. They

walked up to the front desk. The front desk clerk smiled at Sophie.

"Hey, I thought you were off today!"

She nodded. "I am, but Nick brought me here. He said he has

a surprise for me."

The clerk flipped through a book on the counter and nodded.

"Ah, yes. The conference room on the second floor is yours for the

day. Sophie knows the way." They both noticed how the clerk's eyes

lit up when Sophie had said Nick's name and silently wondered who

all Jeff had gossiped to about their involvement.

Nick thanked the clerk and led Sophie to the elevator. They stepped inside and he pressed the button for the second floor. Sophie grinned at him. "Oh come on, tell me!"

He laughed. "We're almost there. Just be patient a little longer."

The elevator stopped at the second floor and the pair stepped out and Nick led her to the conference room. He stopped outside the door and put his hand on the doorknob. "Sophie, what's inside is yours to do with as you wish. But this is my gift to you." He opened the door and they stepped inside.

Sophie's mouth fell open as she stepped into the conference room. The entire room was filled from floor to ceiling with toys! There were bikes, stuffed animals, video games, board games, dolls, footballs, puzzles, and more. Sophie covered her mouth with both hands and took a few steps into the packed room. She turned to look at Nick, her eyes wide, unable to believe what she was seeing. "Nick? What is all this?" Her voice was barely audible as she spoke.

Nick smiled at her. "This is a donation from my company. It's for you to give to the children at the homeless shelter. I have a truck rented to help you get everything to the shelter. We can take

the toys there today if you'd like. If you prefer to wait until

Christmas Eve I can have some men pick up the toys and store them

at the warehouse until then. Just let me know what you prefer."

"Nick…oh my word…thank you so much!" Sophie rushed

over to him and practically launched herself into his arms. "I truly

don't know what to say! The children are going to be so surprised!

Oh, thank you!"

He hugged her tightly. It was very rare that he actually

received thanks for giving someone toys, but he did enjoy that. "My

dear you are ever so welcome."

She released him and looked into his eyes. "Maybe you

really are Santa Claus in disguise. Thank you so much for this!" She

kissed him gently.

His heart swelled at her happiness. He pulled her close and

held her tightly in his arms. "You are so welcome. Now, shall we

deliver these now or store them for Christmas Eve?"

Sophie looked at the mountain of toys. "Let's do wait until

Christmas Eve. There are usually more children at the shelter then and they will be able to benefit from these gifts if we wait. Oh, the kids will be so excited! I can't wait to see their smiling faces!"

Nick nodded and grinned at her. "Me too! That is, if you'll let me come with you to deliver them. Who knows? I might even dress in a Santa suit for it." He winked at her. "Ho ho ho! Do you think I can pass as Santa?"

She laughed. "Oh you could pass for him in your sleep!"

Nick grinned. "As much as I hate to do this, I'll escort you home and then get my men to come collect the toys. Why don't we get together again this evening for dinner?"

Sophie nodded and smiled. "Better yet, it's my turn to give you a gift. Come over at seven and I'll cook you a fabulous dinner. How does that sound?"

"I'd love that! I'll bring the wine." He took her hand and led her back to the elevator.

The walk back to Sophie's apartment was hurried due to the excessive noise of the crowds on the streets. Busy holiday shoppers rushed past others who also were hauling large shopping bags. The sound of taxis rushing by in the slushy roads filled the air. The sounds of cash registers ringing up purchases could be heard coming from the shops as the pair walked. Nick held the door open for her when they arrived and followed her upstairs. They paused outside her door. "Are you sure you can't stay for the rest of the day?" Sophie asked hopefully.

Nick smiled gently and shook his head. "My darling, as much as I would love to I've got to get some work done and get those toys safely to the warehouse. But you'll see me tonight." He gathered her in his arms and kissed her gently. Every time their lips met that seductive jolt of electricity coursed through his veins and he had to struggle not to go further. Reluctantly he ended the kiss and stepped back. "Until tonight, my lady." He planted a soft kiss on the back of her hand and headed back down the stairs.

Momentarily, Nick appeared with a pop in the conference room at the hotel. Kringle was already there with a handful of the elves. "So boss, what's the word? Deliver now or later?"

"Later. She was so excited about the toys and really wants to wait to deliver them till Christmas Eve." Nick watched Kringle as the elderly elf's face turned red.

"By Rudolph's nose, why did we even bring them all the way here if she wanted to wait? This was a huge inconvenience, you know! I had to pull five elves off of the assembly line to just to haul these here, and now we have to haul them back home? What's up with that?" Kringle hopped from one foot to the other in frustration.

"Oh Kringle, calm down. You've moved toys before and it really doesn't take that much elf power. The five elves plus you have more than enough magic to teleport these back to the workshop so stop complaining." Nick wagged a finger at his friend.

Kringle rolled his eyes. "That's beside the point! You think I have nothing better to do than make toys disappear and reappear at your whim? What do I look like?"

Nick grinned. "You look like an elf that has the know-how to get any job done. That's why you're the head elf, you know?"

Kringle bowed low to the ground, a smile emerging on his face. "Of course, you are correct yet again, good sir. I am the best elf for the job, after all." He turned to the other elves. "All right boys, let's put your magic into it and let's get these toys home!" The elves all joined hands and the room glowed bright orange. Instantly the toys disappeared as did the elves. Nick laid his finger aside his nose,

nodded, and also disappeared with the elves and the toys.

Chapter 6

That afternoon Sophie went shopping for the meal she planned to cook for Nick. She decided on Cornish game hen over a bed of garlic-mashed potatoes and paired with grilled asparagus. For dessert she'd whip up a trifle with various berries. It would be a meal fit for a king. She bought the necessary groceries and went home to get started on the preparations for tonight.

She turned on her CD player and popped in some traditional Christmas music. She really wasn't into the remixes of Christmas songs but preferred them to be performed in the traditional manner. She sang along with *O Come, All Ye Faithful* as she rubbed the hen with herbs and spices and popped them into the oven to bake. She diced the potatoes, put them in salted water in a pot, and set the pot on the stove to boil. She checked the clock and headed to her bedroom to decide on an outfit for the evening. She dug through her closet until she came up with a little black dress that hung to her knees but clung to her curves. The neckline was scooped and the sleeves were long and sleek. She laid the dress out on the bed and returned to the kitchen to check on dinner.

Satisfied that everything was coming along well she changed into her dinner clothes and pulled her long hair back into a low ponytail. Sophie returned to the kitchen, tucked a hand towel into the front of her dress, and tied a bath towel around her waist so any little splatters from cooking wouldn't get on her. The oven beeped and she pulled the Cornish game hens out and placed them on the counter to cool. She took a peek at the clock on the stove and realized she only had ten minutes left until Nick was scheduled to arrive.

She quickly heated up the grill plate and popped the asparagus onto it. The potatoes had been boiling so she drained them and dumped the cooked potatoes into a large, yellow Tupperware bowl that has been her mother's before Sophie was even born. She added the garlic and other ingredients and began mashing them by hand. The aroma of the asparagus, Cornish game hens, and the mashed potatoes permeated the entire apartment and made her mouth water. Her arm began aching as she mashed the potatoes. At that exact moment, her doorbell rang. *Crap, I'm not quite ready,* she thought and she rushed over to the door. She opened it quickly. "Hey

Nick, come on in. Sorry I haven't quite finished dinner yet." She

turned back to her asparagus and quickly scooped them off the grill

and onto a serving plate before they burned. Then she returned to

hand mashing the potatoes.

Nick took off his coat and draped it over the couch in the

living room. "It smells like heaven in here! What's cooking?" He

walked up behind her and gently slid his arms around her waist. He

rested his head against her shoulder and softly kissed her neck. "I

missed you today."

Sophie's heart beat faster and she stopped mashing the

potatoes. She turned and found herself face to face with him. "I

missed you too. And dinner tonight is Cornish game hen with

roasted garlic-mashed potatoes and grilled asparagus. I hope you

enjoy it."

He looked down at the towels tucked into her shirt and

around her waist and grinned. "The meal sounds delectable. And I

love the…accessories on your clothes tonight. The dish towel is very

becoming."

She giggled. "I thought you'd like it. Towels are the latest fad." She stepped back and removed the towels. "I just didn't want my dinner clothes to get messed up while finishing the meal. Give me about ten minutes and I'll have the dessert done too. But feel free to stay in the kitchen if you like. Unlike some chefs I don't run people out of my kitchen."

"Oh that's good news! I admit I'm a terrible cook, but I like to watch others in the kitchen. Maybe I'll learn a thing or two." Nick winked at her and stepped back giving her the space she needed to finish the dessert.

Sophie reached into the fridge to get the egg whites, berries, and the rest of the ingredients she needed to make her trifle. While she was layering the berries in the trifle bowls Nick dug through the drawers until he found a corkscrew. "I brought a pinot noir tonight. I wasn't sure what you were planning to cook but it's a very versatile wine. I hope that will be all right."

Sophie grinned. "It's perfect! I love a good pinot noir. Wine glasses are in the cabinet beside the sink."

Nick uncorked the wine and poured two glasses. He took the liberty of setting the table while Sophie finished the trifle. She carefully paid attention to the details of the placement of the hens, potatoes, and asparagus before carrying the plates to the little wooden table. This was definitely not something she did at home often but excelled at it in the kitchen at work.

"Dinner is served," she said and approached her chair. Always the gentleman, Nick held her chair for her and then seated himself.

As the pair cut into their Cornish game hen, Sophie watched Nick's face. He put a bite of the poultry in his mouth and she could tell from his facial expression that he liked the food.

After swallowing that first bite he spoke. "Sophie, you are a miracle worker in the kitchen! I absolutely love this meal."

She grinned. "Why thank you! My years at culinary school paid off then."

He raised his glass. "I'll drink to that!"

They gently clinked the wine glasses together and both took a sip. The pair ate silently for a while, enjoying the delicious meal that

Sophie had prepared for them. In his mind Nick thought *I wonder if she'd cook like this every night!*

In their silence, Nick really studied her face. She had beautiful green eyes that were as deep as emeralds against her creamy complexion. Her dark brown hair hung down her back in waves. Her lips were full and soft. As she closed them around her fork he remembered how their softness turned to passion when they kissed. Her long, slim fingers held her fork and he recalled how well those fingers linked with his as they walked together. She was beautiful, kind, and helpful. She could cook exquisite food and had a heart as beautiful as her face. At that moment, he knew. She was the one. He fell, and fell hard. Watching her eat all he could think about was telling her how much he had fallen in love with her and how he wanted to marry her. But he knew that women needed proof that a man could provide and take care of them.

Of course he could do all of that. He had a rather large workshop at the North Pole. There were thousands of elves there, so she would never be lonely. She seemed to be a person who enjoyed being home and relaxing, so he knew she would be quite comfortable there. Her calm, kind personality would balance out the hyperactive personality of Kringle too. That would be a plus!

What Nick really wished was that he could tell Sophie everything, bring her to the North Pole for a visit, and then pop the question. He thought about asking Kringle if he could break the "no visitors" rule and bring her home to meet everyone. But he could just hear Kringle's high-pitched voice in his mind screaming *no!* over and over.

Would Sophie be happy there with him? She was so close to Mira and she would never see Mira again in person if she chose to accept his proposal and marry him. Would she be all right with that?

His thoughts were interrupted by Sophie's sweet voice speaking to him. "Nick? Is everything all right?"

He was jolted out of his thoughts and brought back to reality. "Oh…yes I'm fine. I was just thinking about something."

Sophie looked at him quizzically. "That was some pretty deep thinking. Are you sure everything's okay? Is the food all right?"

He smiled. "Oh my dear, the food is fantastic!" He finished

the last bite of his mashed potatoes. "I admit as a bachelor I don't get

to eat like this at home. Honestly, I am a terrible cook. The best I

usually do is a can of tomato soup with saltine crackers in it."

Sophie laughed. "Well, you'll just have to come over for

dinner more often." She rose from the table and cleared their plates.

She scraped the bones of the Cornish game hens into the trashcan

and placed the plates in the sink. She opened the cabinet beside the

refrigerator and dug out a couple of bowls. She scooped some of the

trifle into each bowl and returned to the table. "Dessert is served.

Oh, I am sorry, but I forgot to brew coffee. Would you like some?"

Nick shook his head. "Oh no, this will be just fine." As

Sophie sat back down he spoke again. "Truth be told, I never really

developed a taste for coffee. I really prefer hot chocolate."

Sophie nodded. "Ah, I see. That explains why you didn't

order coffee when we went to the coffee shop the other day." She

rose and headed for the pantry. He could hear her rummaging around

and she grabbed a bag of chocolate chips and closed the pantry door.

She reached into the fridge and pulled out a gallon of milk. Then she pulled a pot out of a cabinet and set it on the stove. She added milk,

sugar, and some of the chocolate chips she pulled out of the pantry.

A few minutes later she reached for two coffee mugs and poured the

mixture into it. She added a dollop of whipped cream to the top.

With a smile she returned to the table and set one of the mugs before

Nick. "Homemade hot chocolate. Enjoy!"

As Sophie sat back down Nick took a sip of the hot

chocolate. It was creamy and smooth with just enough sweetness.

"Sophie, this is absolutely excellent hot chocolate!"

She smiled. "Thank you. It's my dad's recipe. During the

winter months he'd make it several times a week. Mom and I always

loved it."

Nick smiled and took a bite of the trifle. The sweet and tart

berries paired with the cream tasted divine. He knew the elves would

love this combination if Sophie were ever able to make it for them.

The pair finished their food and again Sophie cleared the

table. She wrapped her towels around her once again. "One of these

days I'll buy myself an apron and then I won't have to deal with these towels." She giggled as she turned on the water to wash the dishes.

Nick stood and brought the silverware and water glasses to the sink. He set the items down so Sophie could wash them and he picked up a towel from the counter. As she washed a dish she handed it to him. He carefully dried each dish and put it away for her. It wasn't long before the dishes were all washed, dried, and put away. The kitchen was clean once more.

Sophie pulled the towels off of her and dried her wet hands. She dropped the towels on the counter and turned to face him. "I hope you enjoyed dinner."

He smiled and pulled Sophie into his arms. "I did. Thank you." His voice was a whisper as he looked into her eyes. "Sophie..."

She looked up at him and her heart fluttered. He reached up and gently cupped her face with his hands. Slowly he pulled her close and softly placed his lips on hers. She moaned gently and melted against him, fully giving into his kiss. His fingers lightly traced down her back while his lips moved over hers.

Sophie pressed her body against his. He groaned as her breasts pressed against his shirt. He could feel her hardening nipples pressing against his chest. Slowly, he stepped back a little without breaking the kiss. He carefully brought his hands from her back to her sides, gently brushing against the sides of her breasts. She gasped softly. The sound of her gasp sent shivers of delight down his spine. He grew hard and pulled her firmly against him, his hardness pressing into her stomach.

God how he wanted her! It wouldn't take much at all to unzip that lovely dress of hers, take her to bed, and experience the physical pleasure that neither of them had ever experienced. He wanted to do this so badly. And from her reaction to his hardness, she wanted to just as badly.

Again he kissed her, thrusting his tongue into her waiting mouth. She groaned and opened her lips for him. Her hands ran down his back, pulling him firmly against her. Nick reached for her zipper and began slowly unzipping her dress. "Please Nick, hurry…" Sophie gasped, her desire evident in her hushed but anxious tone.

A loud klaxon suddenly interrupted their passionate embrace. They broke their kiss and looked around. Nick quickly zipped Sophie's dress back up and flung open the front door. The sound intensified and flashing strobe lights were going off in the hallway. "Fire alarm," he screamed over the din of the alarm. "We have to go outside." They grabbed their coats, covered their ears, and headed down the stairs with the other residents.

They stood outside with the other people as the fire department responded to the alarm. Two fire trucks came barreling down the road and screeched to a halt in front of the building. Several firemen in their heavy fireproof jackets, pants, and helmets rushed into the building.

The air was chilly and the alarm could still be heard loudly outside. Nick wrapped his arms around her to help keep her warm in the frigid air. She leaned back against him as the firemen shut off the alarm. Nick looked around and saw Kringle's face peering at him through a bush on the other side of the road. He was clearly livid. After about ten minutes they emerged from the building. "All is clear. Looks like someone just pulled the fire alarm. Darn pranksters.

You can all go on back in your apartments now. Sorry about the disruption to your evenings." The firemen all piled back into their trucks and rolled away.

Sophie looked over her shoulder at Nick. "Shall we go back in?" Her tone was hopeful.

Nick smiled, slowly shook his head, and held her tightly. "My dear, we both know what will happen if I go back with you. Perhaps we should call it a night." He gently kissed her cheek. "I know you're working tomorrow, both day and night. Perhaps we can get together in a couple of days?"

Sophie's face fell, but she understood. "Yeah, that will be fine." She snuggled against him and whispered in his ear. "I'm going to have some trouble sleeping tonight though, as I'll be thinking about earlier all night long."

Nick turned and whispered in her ear as well. "You won't be alone in that." He gently nibbled her ear. "Oh my darling, it will happen some day. But we have to slow down for now." He stepped back. "I love you, Sophie. That much is certain."

Her eyes widened. He loved her! Her heart skipped a beat as she replayed his words in her mind. "Oh Nick…" No one had ever said those words to her before.

He smiled at her. "Sleep well, my love. I'll see you in a couple of days." Then he turned and walked across the street. Sophie watched him disappear into the park across the street before she turned and entered the building once more.

Nick watched from the park as Sophie went inside. Then he hurried over to the bush where he had seen Kringle's face. "Come on out, Kringle. I know you're there." Nick heard a pop and Kringle appeared, his face bright red and his eyes narrow. His brow was furrowed and his mouth was twisted into a frown.

Kringle jumped up and down in frustration. "Why?" He was clearly infuriated and could only speak in a few words. "Look, Mr. Claus! You. North Pole. NOW!" Kringle disappeared with a pop after screaming the last word. Nick sighed and followed suit.

The elderly elf and Nick reappeared in Nick's living room. There were two other elves gathered around the scrying bowl that Kringle had obviously been using to keep an eye on them. The two elves looked at one another, looked at Nick, looked at Kringle, gasped and instantly disappeared with a pop.

There was a roaring fire in the red, brick fireplace. The wooden floors were polished. There was a dark red and green rug in the center of the room. The scrying bowl sat in the heart of the rug. The corner of the room held an eight foot tall Christmas tree covered with various ornaments, multi-colored lights, sparkling garland, icicles, and was topped with a beautiful angel with a red velvet dress and glittery white wings. The tree was encircled by a train traveling around a track and whistling merrily as it chugged along. There was a large dark green armchair near the fireplace and the other side held a matching dark green sofa. It was simple and yet cozy.

Kringle hopped up on Nick's armchair and glared at him. "What about staying pure? You're going to mess up the whole prophecy! It's taken hundreds of years for you to find the right woman and you're about to throw away eternal happiness for one wild night of passion?" Kringle grabbed the brightly colored purple beret he was wearing today off his head and hurled it across the room. "You're not married yet! You're extremely close to crossing the line, Mr. Claus! Once you cross it you can't go back again."

Kringle sank to his knees in the chair and Nick sank into the sofa. "I know...I know." Nick's voice was forlorn. Doing the right thing was never, ever easy. He wanted this woman so badly and she wanted him just as much. "I was wrong to do what I did. These feelings are not something I've ever had to handle before. I guess I understand now how difficult it is for people to remain chaste until they get married. That feeling is so carnal, so strong! I never understood it before, but I do now."

Kringle nodded. "Yeah, it is. Why do you think there are so many unwed mothers and pregnant teenagers nowadays? Things aren't the same now as they were two hundred years ago. People marry much later in life now than they did in generations past. But one thing hasn't changed and that's the prophecy. In spite of the carnal desire, you have to remain strong. You have to do the right thing." He hopped off the armchair, jumped right in front of Nick, and pointed a short, stubby finger right at Nick's nose. "Keep your jingle bells housed until you've tied the knot, boss! Got it?"

Nick nodded. "Got it."

Kringle grinned at him. "Good boy. Now go take a snow shower or something. And don't forget, we elves have a knack for knowing who's been naughty and who's been nice! I'd hate to put your name on your own naughty list this year." Kringle bounded out of the room singing at the top of his lungs, "Jingle balls, jingle balls, swinging left and right…"

Chapter 7

Sophie had been quiet all morning. Usually she and Mira were chatting about various topics but for the majority of the morning she was as quiet as a church mouse. She'd done a lot of thinking since the previous night. Physically and emotionally she was ready for the physical acts to take place. She wanted him desperately. She'd never known desire and pure lust before. She'd wanted him to take her to bed and learn the ways of a physical relationship together.

Yet, it seemed like the fire alarm had stopped them both. It was no secret that he wanted her just as much. She remembered his hands on her and longed to feel that again. Yet in spite of the desire, she knew he was right. She'd waited this long already. If Nick was the one for her waiting until their wedding night was the appropriate thing to do.

She was busy cutting dough into the correct portion size for the crust of several individual chicken pot pies when Mira's voice broke the silence. "Soph, you seem so distracted today. Are you going to tell me about it? What happened last night?"

Sophie sighed and set down the knife she was using to slice the dough. "Well…things took a turn down the carnal path."

Mira gasped. "And? Did you do it?"

Sophie shook her head. "No, but I wanted to. God, I wanted to! But someone pulled the fire alarm and we all got evacuated from the building for about fifteen minutes until all was clear. It was probably some punk kid playing a prank but it royally screwed up my evening. Honestly we had just begun to undress when the alarm sounded!" She balled her hand into a fist and slammed it down on the counter. "Why is it that every time we start to get physical something happens to stop it? For goodness sake, this is my first experience with a man and I want to experience it all! Why in the world is this not happening?"

Mira looked at the frustration on Sophie's face. "Well…after the fire alarm was done did you go back to your apartment and continue where you left off?"

Sophie shook her head. "No, he said it was best if we didn't and left." She sighed. "Mira…why is chastity so darn important to him? We both were totally ready until that stupid fire alarm went off. Then it's like…all of a sudden he totally changed his mind and went back to being Mr. Nothing Physical! That's frustrating, in more way than one."

Mira nodded. "No kidding! I'd be frustrated too. But, maybe he's right. You've shown him that you're interested. You've pushed the envelope, so to speak. But apparently he's not ready. Remember, like I told you before he's from a different generation. He apparently takes things slower. Maybe right now you two shouldn't focus on the physical desires that you both obviously have. Focus on relationship building. Learn about his likes and dislikes. Find out if you really love him or if you just lust for him."

Sophie nodded. "Oh, and speaking of love…he told me he loved me last night. Can you believe it? There's a guy in this world who really and truly loves me!"

Mira grinned. "I knew it! That's totally amazing!" She clasped her hands together. "You definitely need to focus on the love and affection right now then. Build on that. Experience different things together. He's a gentleman. Let him show you what it's like to be courted by a gentleman. Honey, there are so few of them left in this world now that finding one is a rare gem. Do fun things together. Visit the theater or the ballet. Go to an opera. Let him wine and dine you. And through it all you'll learn about him. You'll find out what interests him. Learn about his likes and dislikes. Find out what makes him tick. Believe me, that will be a challenge but fun at the same time."

Sophie smiled at her friend. "Mira, for as much as you know about dating it's a miracle you're not married with fifteen kids yet."

Mira howled with laughter. "Oh I don't want to get married yet! I just want to live it up and enjoy life right one. Oh sure someday I may bite the bullet and tie the knot with someone, but for now I'm happy as I am."

Sophie turned back to her dough. "I thought I was too. But honestly, I didn't know what I was missing. I am really enjoying the company. I never knew I was lonely until now."

As she went back to working with her dough Sophie though about her life and realized that deep down inside she had been lonely ever since her parents died. She had been completely alone with no family and only Mira as a friend. Even after work Sophie had always been a homebody. She wasn't a party girl, didn't go out to clubs, and didn't get drunk. She went to work, came home, and relaxed. Lather, rinse, and repeat. This was her life. She was predictable and lived a very routine life. She realized that she'd never been on an amusement park ride. She'd never gone swimming in the ocean. She'd never gone ice skating. Ever since the death of her parents she'd sheltered herself from the world and consequently sheltered her heart as well.

Having no people in her life meant having no pain. It had worked quite well until now. She knew now that a big part of life was having someone to share it with. She was beginning to think that maybe the ups and down of life was what made living so worth it. There could be no real pleasure without experiencing a little plain as well. She wasn't experiencing those peaks and valleys. Everything was predictable and routine for her. For once in her life, Sophie

realized that she was missing something.

"Mira? Be honest with me. Did you ever look at me and

think that I was lonely?" Sophie's voice was quiet as she asked her

question.

Mira stopped working and looked over at her friend.

"Honestly, yes. You never varied your routine. Wake up, come to

work, go home, chill out, and go to bed. Over and over and over

again. That was your life. Occasionally you and I would go out and

grab dinner but that was really it. You always seemed too reserved

and never really connected with a lot of people. I always just thought

you were a bit of an introvert until we got to know each other. Then I

knew that you were alone in the world." Mira walked over to Sophie

and put a hand on her shoulder. "But you've got me. And now

you've got Nick."

"What about the age thing? It clearly doesn't bother him and

it doesn't bother me. Do you think other people will have issues with

that? I mean he's nearly double my age." Sophie's green eyes met

Mira's.

Mira shrugged. "What does that matter? Who gives a care what other people think about it? He doesn't act like an old man. From what I could see, he's smitten with you. He loves you for who you are. The question now is...do you love him for who he is?"

Sophie paused and then nodded. "Yes. I wouldn't change him for anything. He's an amazing man."

Mira smiled. "There you go! See, it really is simple. Love is what it is. Enjoy it for what it is and stop over thinking things."

That night after the show Sophie walked home alone. This would be the first night in a week that she hadn't seen Nick. She couldn't get him out of her mind. She hoped with each step that he'd come out of nowhere and go home with her. But as she entered her small apartment, she knew she was alone. She wasn't sure where he was today. She just knew that she missed him and wanted to be with him.

Inside her small apartment she changed out of her work clothes and put on a pair of pajama pants and an old t-shirt. She headed to the kitchen and microwaved herself a bag of popcorn. She sank onto her old brown couch and turned on the TV with the press of a button. She turned on the Hallmark Channel and was soon

entranced by a Christmas special.

After the bag of popcorn was finished and the movie

followed suit she checked the clock and realized it was after ten. She

really needed to get to bed. She switched off the TV and headed off

to bed. She was looking forward to seeing Nick tomorrow.

That same night, Nick was lying in bed back at the North

Pole. His bedroom was extremely large and held a wooden four-

poster bed with a bright red comforter and satin pillows. There was a

small fireplace in the corner of the room that illuminated the bed and

the night tables. One held his Santa hat and had a small alarm clock

on it. The other night table was completely bare. He looked over at

that table and thought of Sophie. He imagined the night when she

would lay her own hat on that table and have a clock there of her

own.

He thought of her and wondered how she did today. He

intentionally had stayed away from Quebec. He remained at the

North Pole the entire day. Kringle hadn't let him out of his sight. He

worked on the naughty and nice list, checked on the workshop, saw to it that toy production would go into overtime to meet the demand of all of the good little girls and boys this year, and examined each and every reindeer to make sure each one was in tip top shape and ready for Christmas Eve.

It was a busy day and one that he had needed. Spending a day away from Sophie was tough but it cemented in his mind and in his heart that she was the one for him. His thoughts were constantly on her, wondering what she was doing and how she was feeling. He wondered if she was feeling the same way he was at that moment. Here he was, laying in bed and his thoughts were on this beautiful woman that he loved with all of his heart. He only could hope that he would earn her love in return.

Chapter 8

After Sophie got off work she hurried out the door of the hotel. To her happiness, there was Nick waiting for her. She smiled and hurried over to him. He held out his hand and took her hand in his. "I've missed you and thought about you ever since the fire alarm." He leaned over and gently kissed her.

She nodded and gently squeezed his hand. "And I've thought about you as well. I went to bed last night wishing that I had a number where I could call you."

Nick smiled. "Believe it or not, I don't even have a cell phone. I've never needed one."

Sophie cocked her had to one side. "You are a businessman without a cell phone? Well what about an e-mail address? Do you carry a laptop with you?"

He shook his head. "Nope. No computer of any kind. I may be a bit old fashioned but I just use a pen and paper for my business."

Sophie was flabbergasted. How could anyone in business in this day and age not be using computers or a cell phone? "But…how does that work?"

He winked at her. "One day I'll show you. But today's not that day. Tell me something. I want to know something that you've always wanted to do but have never done in your life. If I can make it happen, I'll do it. So tell me something you'd like to do."

Sophie thought for a moment and then smiled. "Well, there are two things. I've never been on a Ferris wheel and I've never been ice skating."

Nick nodded. "Ah, I see. Well, unfortunately there are no Ferris wheels in Quebec at this time of year. But I do know of a pond where we could go ice skating. It's on the edge of town. Let's catch a taxi." He stepped over to the curb and flagged down a passing cab. They both climbed in and Nick gave the driver an address. The cab pulled away from the curb and Nick slipped his arm around Sophie's shoulders.

She leaned against him enjoying the feel of his arm around her. He always smelled heavenly in a way that just made her happy.

The scent reminded her of a combination between peppermint and pine. There was something very comforting about it and she leaned closer to him, inhaling. She wondered what cologne he used and vowed silently to examine his bathroom counter to find out if she ever visited his hotel room.

The cab traveled the busy streets for about twenty minutes until it came to a stop at the edge of town. There was a small pond that had completely iced over. There were a handful of people skating on the pond. They saw a mother and father each holding the hands of a little boy who was having trouble staying on his feet. They saw a couple of teenage girls racing around the pond trying to skate faster than the other. There was a small shack near the pond with a man inside. A sign on the shack offered to rent stakes for a small fee. Nick approached the shack and paid the man for two pairs of skates. After asking their sizes the man handed over the pairs of skates to Nick and Sophie.

They sat down on a very cold bench near the pond to put their skates on. Nick deftly laced his up while Sophie struggled with how loose or tight to lace hers. He leaned over and helped her lace up the skates. "They need to be firm but not too tight. We don't want

to cut off the circulation but still want them to be tight enough to

support your ankles." He helped her to her feet and slowly they

made their way down to the pond.

Nick stepped onto the ice and held his hand out to Sophie.

Hesitantly she took his hand and stepped out onto the ice. It was very

slippery and she felt her feet going right out from under her. Nick

grabbed her and pulled her against him. She laughed as he caught

her and he began laughing too. "The trick to skating is to go slowly

at first. If you've ever roller skated it's similar but you have to

balance sideways as well as front and back. It's not easy but it's a lot

of fun once you get the hang of it. Just take it easy and relax. I've got

you."

Very carefully Sophie began to glide across the ice holding

Nick's hand. Her feet felt very unsteady but soon she was beginning

to get the hang of it. She used the little grooves at the front of the toe

to stop herself if she felt unsure and then would push off as if skiing

to get going again. The wind whipped past her as the pair of racing teenage girls flew by and she laughed. "I'll never be as quick as they are."

Nick laughed too. "You don't have to be. Just have fun with it." He held her hand and the pair slowly skated side by side.

Sophie looked over at Nick who was able to skate with no trouble at all. "How did you get so good at this?"

He winked at her. "I learned when I was a boy and never lost the skill. I go skating every winter and I enjoy it tremendously. I'll tell you a secret. I never learned to ride a bike but this was the closest thing to it for me. I can go as fast as I want to and stop on a dime. It's reckless but fun."

Sophie began to go a little faster and Nick easily stayed with her. They glided across the ice smoothly going in a circle around the little pond. As they moved the little boy who had been skating with his parents called out, "Mommy! I see Santa Claus!"

Both Nick and Sophie giggled. Nick said, "I think I'll play along and go ask the young man what he wants for Christmas." He released Sophie's hand. "Will you be all right?"

She nodded. "Absolutely I've got this." Slowly she skated off and let Nick go over to the little boy. She slowly made her way around the pond as Nick knelt down beside the boy and his mother. He spoke only to the boy and the boy was clearly enamored with Nick. She smiled as she could see the boy excitedly talking to Nick. He was really good with kids.

Night had fallen and two more skaters had joined the people on the ice. These skaters were two young teenage boys; both were wearing black skates with bright neon green laces and carried glow-in-the-dark hockey sticks. The boys dropped a puck on the ice and began to play.

Sophie moved away from the boys to give them more room to play their game. She watched Nick and the little boy talk. Then the little boy gave Nick a hug. Nick ruffled the boy's hair, smiled up at the boy's mom, and began to head back toward Sophie. "What did you say to him?" she asked Nick when he reached her.

Nick smiled. "That's between me and him, my love. But he told me what he wanted for Christmas. Hopefully Santa will be able to help him out."

The teenage boys whizzed past Nick and Sophie engrossed in their hockey game. "Careful boys," Nick called out but the boys paid him no attention. They raced around the pond stealing the puck from one another and then racing to the other side of the pond again. Sophie and Nick were in the center of the pond when the boys came straight at them. Nick was able to dodge but Sophie didn't get out of the way in time. The boys slammed straight into her. They knocked her flat on the ground and she slid rapidly across the ice. She finally stopped sliding fifteen feet away.

Sophie lay on the ice as the boys got up. "Sorry!" they called before resuming their game. A crackling sound suddenly resounded all around Sophie. She gasped as she realized spider-web cracks were appearing all around her. "Nick!" she screamed. "The ice is breaking!"

"Sophie!" Nick cried out as the ice gave way and Sophie sank into the crackling ice. He heard her cry out before she sank beneath the freezing water.

The absolutely freezing temperature of the water completely took Sophie's breath away as she sank beneath the surface. It was dark outside but she could see the glimmer of lights through the ice above her. She struggled to get to the surface but the heavy ice skates impeded her swimming. She looked up and she could see the hole that she had sank through about two feet above her. She continued to sink slowly. She couldn't hold her breath any longer and exhaled. As she inhaled the icy water filled her lungs. She tried to cough but it did her no good. She struggled and kicked with all of her might but continued to sink beneath the icy water. Her vision grew dim and she began to give in to the feeling of impending death. As the lights began to go out she was faintly aware of the sound of a loud splash. As she closed her eyes she felt someone grab her arm. Then the world faded to blackness.

Chapter 9

Nick's fingers closed around her arm and he hauled her out of the freezing water. The other skaters had moved to the edge of the pond. Several were clearly frightened and one man held a cell phone to his ear. Nick was half soaked but he didn't care. He dragged Sophie off the ice and onto the frozen ground. Her lips were blue and her eyes were closed, lifeless. Nick leaned down and listened for her breathing but heard nothing. He did several chest compressions and checked again to see if she was breathing. "Please, someone call an ambulance!" he screamed as he continued chest compressions and breathed into her lungs.

Within a moment he heard the sirens of the ambulance as it barreled down the street toward the pond. The vehicle screeched to a halt by the pond, sirens blaring and red and white lights flashing. Two paramedics leaped from the vehicle and rushed to Sophie's side. "She fell through the ice," Nick cried as he moved aside to let them do their work. They scooped her up and carried her to the ambulance and loaded her onto a gurney. Nick followed quickly and climbed into the ambulance with her. Then the paramedics slammed the doors and sped away.

The ride to the hospital was very surreal for Nick. Even though he was there and was answering questions about Sophie and the accident to the paramedics he felt like he was an observer, watching the events through someone else's eyes. They arrived at the hospital rapidly and the paramedics wheeled Sophie into the emergency room. The doctor and two nurses met them and the paramedics rattled off the information that Nick had given them. One of the nurses stopped Nick. "Sir, you won't be able to go with her. Come with me and I'll show you to the waiting room," she said gently.

Nick's heart sank as he watched the gurney being wheeled behind a door that he wasn't allowed to cross. He sighed and followed the nurse to the waiting room. He filled out some basic paperwork so they would know who she was, sank into a chair, and waited for news. A moment later Kringle came walking through the emergency room door and into the waiting room. He sat down somberly in a chair next to Nick. Kringle was dressed to blend in this time, wearing a small gray coat, long black pants, and a matching charcoal gray hat. "I saw what happened but couldn't do anything to stop it," he mumbled. "I'm sorry."

Nick nodded. "There was nothing I could do either." His voice wavered as he spoke. "Will she be all right?"

Kringle shrugged. "I don't know but I hope so. I want her to be all right."

The pair sat in silence and waited for news. They watched as people came and went, patients arrived and were released, and others in the waiting room got up to go with them. Hours passed and finally a doctor came to the waiting room and approached Nick and Kringle. "Sir, Sophie's stable. She's in a coma." The doctor knelt down so he could look into Nick's eyes. "I don't know how long she'll be unconscious…or if she will wake up. She was under the water for several minutes and may have suffered some brain damage from it. She's being moved to intensive care. You can go up to see her if you like but won't be allowed to stay for more than ten minutes tonight as visiting hours are over."

Nick nodded. "Yes…I'd like to see her." The doctor nodded. She's in room four in the ICU. Go on up. The nurse will let you in."

As the doctor walked away Nick turned to Kringle. "Brain damage? Coma? Good Lord…she's…will she make it?" His shaking voice was barely audible.

Kringle, for once, had no comment. He could only look at Nick with uncertainty in his eyes. The pair got up and headed for the ICU. The nurse buzzed Nick in and said that only one visitor was permitted. Kringle waited outside for Nick.

Nick walked down the hallways of the intensive care unit. The rooms were all large and filled with extremely sick patients. He reached room four and entered. There was Sophie. She was clearly hooked up to a breathing machine. Several blankets covered her body. Her eyes were closed and her chest rose and fell with the machine as it rhythmically pumped air into her lungs.

Nick walked over to the bed and took Sophie's freezing hand in his. Her hand had no warmth, no life. He gently squeezed hers but got no returning squeeze. A lump formed in his throat. He sank to his knees and clasped his hands together, holding her hand between

118

them. He closed his eyes and prayed earnestly for help in saving the woman that he loved. Nick prayed fervently until the nurse returned and told him it was time to go but that he could come back tomorrow morning.

He rose, wiped the tears from his face and laid Sophie's hand down on the bed. He reached out and gently stroked her cheek. "I'll be back tomorrow, my love. Stay strong, rest, and I will see you then." Reluctantly, he turned and allowed the nurse to escort him out of the ICU.

Kringle and Nick both magically whisked themselves back to the North Pole and reappeared in Nick's living room. The scrying bowl was still in the middle of the floor. Nick sank into his armchair. "Kringle, we have all the magic in the world, but we can't even use it to save her life? We can't ensure that she'll be okay? What good is magic if we can't use it to save the people we love?"

Kringle sighed. "Nick, just because we have been given the gift of magic doesn't mean we are allowed to do everything. There are still miracles in this world that even Santa and his elves can't fix. That's where the real 'Big Guy' comes in. You were right to pray for her. I did the same while you were in her room. Go back and see her tomorrow but for now, rest and pray. That's all you can do right now."

Nick rose from the couch and shuffled up the stairs and down the hallway to his bedroom. He changed into his nightclothes and dropped his regular clothes in a pile on a chair in the corner of the room. He stood beside his bed with a heavy heart. He sank to his knees, folded his hands, and began to pray for Sophie's health. "Dear Lord, please...please heal her. I've lived for far too long without someone like her in my life and I don't want to lose her now. Please let her be all right."

Back at the hospital Sophie remained in a coma. She was still, yet her mind was active. She could hear those around her faintly but wasn't able to respond to them. She wasn't sure why. She suddenly felt like she was floating. She looked around and could see the hospital room. She looked down and saw her body lying below on the bed. She faintly heard the machines beeping and fading to a flat line below, but she didn't really care. She saw a doctor and a couple of nurses rush into her room. All of her cold and pain faded away. She drifted upward through the ceiling and into darkness. She felt like she was in a dark tunnel and she saw a faint light far ahead and began to float toward the light. Suddenly a voice stopped her.

"Sophia? My little Sophia, is that really you?"

Sophie froze as she heard the familiar voice. "Papa? Is that you?"

"Yes, sweetheart it's me." She couldn't see him but very clearly heard her father's voice speaking to her from that light. "You must stop though. Go back. It's not your time. Besides there's a man down there who won't be able to live without you."

Sophie spoke. "Papa? You know about Nick?"

Her father spoke back, his voice echoing through the darkness. "Yes, I know about Nick. And before you ask, your mother and I definitely approve. He's a good man and will love you for the rest of time. That's all we could ever want for you. We know more about him than you do at this point."

Sophie replied frantically as she felt her soul being tugged toward her body. "You do? Tell me everything! I want to know about him!"

Her father's voice began to fade away, as did the light at the end of that dark tunnel. "He's the one for you. That's all you need to know for now. We love you but it's time to go back. We love you so much, Sophie. But you have to be with him now. Go back and know that we will always love you."

Sophie felt a jolt and suddenly felt like she was falling through the sky. As she began to get dizzy from the falling sensation she found herself back on the bed and in her body once more. Her eyes flew open and she felt tremendous pain like a thousand needles stabbing into her body. She gasped and coughed, pulling the breathing tube from her throat. She gagged a bit as the foreign object was removed. "Wait, wait Sophie!" A nurse called her name. "You have to relax."

Sophie threw the blankets off and tried to crawl out of the bed. "Nick! I have to find Nick." Two more nurses rushed into the room. One reached out and took Sophie's trembling hand and patted it.

"Sleep now, Sophie. You'll see your guest in the morning." The other nurse's voice was calm as she injected something into Sophie's IV.

Sophie felt the medication wash over her body and before she knew it, she fell into a deep sleep.

The next morning Nick was there right as visiting hours began. The nurse escorted him to Sophie's room. "Last night she came out of her coma. I think she's on the road to recovery now. She's not out of the woods yet but being awake is a great sign."

The nurse let Nick enter Sophie's room on his own. As he entered he looked over at the bed with hopeful eyes. She was still lying still with her eyes closed. He walked over to the bed and covered her hand with his own. "Sophie? Can you hear me?"

She flinched and her eyes fluttered. Slowly, she opened them and she looked up into Nick's face. "Nick," she whispered softly. "Are you really here?"

Nick breathed a sigh of relief and sat down on the edge of her bed. "Yes my love, I'm really here."

She sat up weakly and Nick gathered her into his arms.

"Thank God you're all right." Tears of relief poured out of his eyes and onto her shoulder as he held her. "Sophie, I was terrified that I'd lost you forever when you sank under that water."

She snuggled close against his chest. "I was afraid of that too. I don't want to lose you. I love you."

He sighed, his heart leaping in his chest. She loved him too! He couldn't believe it! She loved him and he loved her!

The nurse came in. "And how are you feeling this morning? Hopefully you are much better." She was carrying some medicine and a stethoscope. Nick released Sophie so the nurse could check her vital signs and Sophie could take the medicine the nurse had brought. "We've got an MRI scheduled for later today to assess any potential problems you may have in your brain. But based on what I'm seeing here, you'll pass that with no trouble. Hopefully in a couple of days you'll be able to go home."

The nurse left and Nick pulled her into his arms once more. "I can't tell you how grateful I am that you're all right. We'll let the doctors do their tests but I am sure they will find that you are just fine."

The tests that afternoon yielded good results and Sophie was moved out of ICU and into a regular room. That evening while Nick and Sophie were sitting in her room Mira came by.

"Hey! Nick called the hotel and let me know you were going to be all right. I was so relieved to hear the good news!" Mira was carrying a large brown paper bag. "I brought dinner if you're hungry. Tonight we had a wedding buffet and I brought some leftovers. There's ham, pasta, green beans, dinner rolls with butter, and I even managed to snag three pieces of wedding cake for dessert." She reached into the bag and brought out the white foam take-out containers. She also pulled out a handful of plastic eating utensils and some napkins.

The three sat and ate the tasty dinner. "Thanks for bringing food Mira. I tell you, this hospital food is so bland compared to what I normally cook. It could really use some seasoning." She took a bite of the sweet ham. "So delicious!"

Mira turned to Nick. "I can't thank you enough for being there to pull her out of the water. She's my best friend and I just don't know how I would have handled it if she hadn't made it. I really owe you one, Nick. Thanks."

The three people finished their dinner and Nick rose. "I'll get these containers out of here. I should probably head home for the night." He leaned over and gently kissed Sophie. "I'll see you tomorrow." He put all of the containers into the large brown paper bag. "Good night, Mira, and thanks for the dinner."

"Anytime!" Mira replied.

Nick smiled. He picked up the bag and with one last look at Sophie he headed out of the room.

Sophie listened as Nick's footsteps faded as he walked away from her room. "Oh Mira, he's an amazing man." She leaned back into her pillow and pulled the blanket up to her chin. "Something happened after I fell in the water."

Mira flopped down on the foot of the hospital bed. "Really? What happened?"

Sophie spoke quietly. "I think I died."

Mira's eyes widened. "Why would you say that?"

Sophie sighed. "Well, I was in pain and then suddenly I felt no pain at all. I could see my body below me. I went right through the ceiling and was in this really dark tunnel. I saw a light, just like I've heard happens when someone dies. And then I heard my dad's voice. He was telling me that it wasn't my time and that I had to go back. Then I felt this pulling and I literally felt like my spirit was dumped back into my body." She paused and took a deep breath. "The whole experience was really weird. But my dad talked about Nick. He told me Nick was the right man for me and that he and mom both approved of him."

Mira smiled. "Wow, that's pretty amazing! If that really was your dad, it's fantastic that he and your mom approve of Nick."

Sophie nodded, rolled over, and propped herself up on one elbow. "It's not just that, Mira. Nick's special. I…okay you're going to think I'm insane, but do you believe in Santa Claus?"

Mira's brow furrowed and she shrugged. "That's a weird question, you know. But no, not in the literal sense. Why?"

Sophie nodded. "Yeah, I know. But there have been some things that have happened that make me think there's more to him than he's letting on."

"Like what?" Mira's curiosity got the best of her. She crossed her legs as she sat on the foot of the bed, propped her elbows on her knees, and rested her chin in her hands.

"Well, he's told me that he's in the toy business and that he was in town for some business deal. I honestly don't know of any toy manufacturers in our town. I haven't researched it or anything, but I just don't think there are any." Sophie sighed.

Mira replied, "Well, that doesn't make him Santa Claus. Maybe he just doesn't want you to know about his background yet. He may be some sort of government spy or something. You never know."

"That's exactly it. I've never been one to be totally open about myself or my own background. And yet, from the minute I met him I felt totally comfortable with him. I've never had any problem talking to him about anything. I've told him about my parents. And he knows about me donating toys to the kids at the homeless shelter each year." Sophie paused. "Do you know what he did?"

Mira shook her head. "No. What did he do?"

"Well," Sophie continued, "he gave me several hundred toys a few days ago! You know that big conference room on the second floor at the hotel? It was packed full of toys! The table, the floor... it was all full of toys! He brought them to me as a donation for the kids."

Mira's eyes widened. "Holy cow! That's a lot of toys! That's really kind of him. But there's no way all of those would fit in your second bedroom. Where are they now?"

"He took them back to his warehouse supposedly. We're going to deliver them together on Christmas Eve." Sophie paused again. "Warehouse? Or workshop? I bet he really took the toys back to his home at the North Pole."

Mira laughed. "Sophie, you are making way too much of this. You really think your boyfriend is Santa Claus? I mean, sure he looks the part. Maybe he's a mall Santa in his spare time or on weekends or something. But the real deal? Honey, I hate to break it to you but there is no Santa Claus."

Sophie sighed. "There's more. He's magic. He tried to hide it, but I know he has magic."

Mira rolled her eyes. "Okay, so maybe he's a Wiccan or a Pagan."

Now it was Sophie's turn to laugh. "Oh no, he believes in God. He's not a Wiccan or a Pagan. I'm certain of that. I've heard him pray before. But, there was one time we were going to go out and my hair was wet. My back was to him and my hair suddenly went from wet to dry. I questioned it and he claims that maybe the air vent was blowing hot air at the right angle or something. But I swear, I know it was him. Just before it happened he asked me if I was going to dry my hair and I told him no. He didn't want me to go out with it wet so apparently he dried it himself. How? I have no idea. But I swear, he did."

"He dried your hair?" Mira cocked her head to one side. "Soph, this sounds so ridiculous."

"I know!" Sophie's excitement was evident in her tone. "It makes no sense. But there's one other thing. He disappeared."

"He…what?" Mira looked confused. "How could he disappear?"

"I have no idea. One night he was leaving my apartment. I watched him go into the stairwell. I went to the window to watch him leave the building but he never came out. I have no idea where he went but it's just like he disappeared into thin air."

"Okay, let me get this straight. He dried your hair. He disappeared. He gave you a whole truckload of toys. And he has a long white beard. So you think he's Santa Claus? Sophie, maybe you still have a concussion or some sort of brain damage from your ordeal under the ice. How can I explain this? There is no Santa Claus!" Mira looked into her friend's eyes. "Get it?"

Sophie sighed. "I knew you wouldn't believe me. Mira, maybe he's not Santa Claus…but he's not just some regular guy. He's definitely special. He just…seems so Santa-like. Even his name is Nick. Like Nicholas. Saint Nicholas. Otherwise known as Santa Claus?"

"Oh Sophie, there are thousands of guys named Nick in this world. Are every single one of them really Santa Claus in disguise?" Mira shook her head. "No, it's just a name." She stood up. "It's late and it's clear you aren't right in the head at the moment. Get some rest and we'll talk again tomorrow." She leaned over and hugged Sophie. "See you later."

Mira left the hospital room and left Sophie to her own thoughts. Mira definitely didn't believe her. That didn't surprise Sophie. She didn't think Mira would believe her. After all, very few people over the age of twelve believed in Santa Claus. Still, Sophie believed. She didn't know how she would prove it, but in her heart she believed that her boyfriend Nick was really and truly Santa Claus.

Chapter 10

The doctors finally agreed to let Sophie go home. Nick and Mira both met Sophie at the hospital to take her back to her apartment. Mira had a cab waiting outside to give them a ride back. The orderly wheeled Sophie out of the hospital and Nick helped her into the cab.

On the ride back to her apartment Sophie was elated to finally be free of the hospital. "I can't tell you both how glad I am to be out of there! I thought I was going to go nuts if I had to spend another day in that room." She sighed and leaned back into the seat of the cab.

Mira laughed. "I understand that! But you still have some recovery time left. Remember, the doctors said you had to rest at home for four days before you could return to work."

Sophie nodded. "Yeah, I know. I'll definitely prefer to relax at home instead of that hospital though. It will be nice to be back in my own space."

The ride back to her apartment only took about fifteen minutes. The cab let the threesome out right at the front door. Nick took Sophie's arm and gently guided her up the stairs. He didn't want to risk her falling just as she got home. Mira unlocked Sophie's door and the group entered.

"Home sweet home," Sophie exhaled as she entered her apartment. "I didn't know I could miss this place so much."

Mira nodded. "That's the truth! Well as much as I hate to do this I have to run. My shift starts in an hour and I've got to get over to the hotel. There's some prep work I need to do for the banquet tonight. Some office party is hosting a dinner in the ballroom and I've got lots of slicing and dicing for the salad bar to get done. Will you be all right without me?"

Sophie smiled at her friend. "Oh, I think I can manage. Besides, Nick's here so I'm not alone."

Mira hugged her friend. "Okay. Just call me if you need anything at all." She released Sophie and turned to Nick. "Take care of her, all right? Don't let her do anything too wild."

Nick laughed heartily. "Okay, no ice skating or rock climbing tonight. I promise."

Mira laughed as well. "See you folks later." She headed out the door and closed it behind her.

Nick turned to Sophie. "Welcome home, my dear." He sidled up behind her and wrapped his arms around her. He pulled her against his chest and buried his face into her neck. "I can't tell you how glad I am that you're home and out of the hospital. I was so worried about you."

Sophie sighed and leaned back against Nick. She snuggled against him enjoying the feel of his arms around her. "Me too. I really missed being here with you. I mean, it was fantastic that you came to see me while I was in the hospital but I like us being here even better."

Nick gently kissed her neck and released her. "I do too." He led Sophie over to the couch, picked up the remote, and turned on the television. He flipped through channels until he found *It's a Wonderful Life* on. "Oh, this is one of my favorites. Let's watch it."

The pair sank into the couch and Nick wrapped an arm around Sophie. The both watched as the movie played. Nick began randomly quoting lines of the movie eliciting a laugh from Sophie each time he quoted funny lines and a smile as he quoted profound ones. "Sorry, I hope you don't mind. This is one of my personal favorites though."

She smiled. "Oh, I don't mind at all. It's a great movie." She was enjoying just being with him.

After the movie ended Nick turned down the volume on the television. "Tell me something Sophie. We only have a couple of weeks left until Christmas. Why haven't you decorated your apartment yet?" His bright eyes focused on hers.

She sighed. "Well, ever since my parents died I haven't decorated."

Nick cocked his head to one side. "Why not?"

"Well, it's just me," replied Sophie. "Since I work on Christmas and don't have any presents to open there's no sense in putting up a tree or decking my halls. I don't have the storage space to store a fake tree year round and I don't see the sense in killing one every year just for a couple of weeks worth of decorating."

"You really don't decorate at all?" Nick was quite surprised.

Sophie shook her head. "Nope. It's not that I have anything against Christmas. I just don't have family to share it with and there's no sense in doing it for just me." She looked into Nick's eyes. "Is Christmas your favorite holiday?"

He nodded. "Absolutely! It's a toy maker's dream every year! Christmas is the best time of year. People are merry. There are decorations everywhere. Everyone's singing carols. There's peace on earth and good will toward men. Jesus' birth is celebrated. Children are filled with excitement at what's under the tree and ponder what they will find in their stockings on Christmas morning. What's not to love about Christmas? It's the most wonderful time of the year."

Sophie nodded. "That's all very true."

Nick got an idea for a surprise for her but he didn't want to give it away. He reached out and gently placed his hand on her

137

shoulder. "My dear, you must be exhausted. You should lie down and take a nap for a bit."

Sophie shook her head. "I'm not tired one bit."

Nick's bright eyes seemed to be smiling at her and she felt one of his fingers trace up the base of her neck. "Yes, you are."

Instantly Sophie yawned. "Hmmm…maybe you are right. Maybe I will lie down for a bit."

Nick guided her to her bedroom. The wooden floor was covered in a bright blue rug. The bed was topped with a matching blue comforter and was covered in white and blue throw pillows. There was a small settee near the window and a vanity on the opposite wall. Nick tossed the throw pillows onto the settee and turned down the covers for Sophie. She crawled into bed. "Now close your eyes my love."

Sophie glanced at the clock and then closed her eyes and Nick placed a hand on her forehead. "Sleep, my darling. Sleep until I awaken you." Instantly, her breathing changed and she was fast asleep. Nick smiled and walked back into the living room. "Kringle? I know you can hear me. Come here."

POP! Instantly, Kringle was there. "What? How did you know I happened to be checking in on you at that very moment?"

Nick laughed. "Because I know you! You are so interested in what's happening that you can't stay away from that scrying bowl."

Kringle giggled. "That much is true. This is better than a soap opera! Now, what can old Kringle do for you?"

Nick motioned to the room. "What's missing in this space?"

"Um…" Kringle paused and looked around. "There are no deer heads or fish on the walls?"

"No, smart aleck," Nick replied in an exasperated tone. "This whole place is devoid of Christmas decorations."

"Oh, you're right. Maybe we could hang a deer head on the wall and deck out his antlers? Or what about hanging a fish head on the wall? That's different!"

Nick rolled his eyes. "Nope. That's not happening. But we really could help Sophie out and get her more in the spirit of things. Let's decorate. We can put a tree over by the window. Let's string some garland across the windows and put a wreath on the door. Lights can be strung around the windows and we can put those pretty candle lights in the windows too. I'd love to put a little Christmas spirit into her apartment. What do you think?"

Kringle snapped his fingers and instantly ten different sport fish were hanging on the wall over Sophie's television. "There! Fish heads!" Kringle snapped his fingers and the fish all began singing Dr. Demento's *Fish Heads* song. Kringle heartily joined in.

Nick groaned. "Kringle, you lunatic! I told you, no fish heads! And no song!" He snapped his fingers and the fish disappeared and the song ceased.

"Spoil sport," Kringle muttered. He sighed. "All right, one festively decorated apartment coming up!"

Kringle began waving his hands and snapping his fingers. Immediately decorations began appearing out of nowhere. Nick directed Kringle where to place them and within minutes Sophie's entire apartment was decorated for Christmas. "This is perfect Kringle! Now I need to go wake her up. Thanks for your help."

"Sure, no problem Boss. I didn't have much choice in the matter, but I hope she likes it. I still think we should have the fish heads though!" Kringle grinned.

"No fish heads!" Nick exclaimed.

Kringle cackled with laugher before disappearing with a pop.

Nick walked back down the short hallway to Sophie's bedroom. He waved his hand slowly over her eyes. "Awaken, my love." His voice was calm as Sophie's eyes fluttered open.

"Oh, I guess I took a power nap or something." She stretched and sat up. She glanced at the clock and realized that only about fifteen minutes had passed since she had lain down.

He smiled gently. "Oh that's just fine. It let me do a little something for you." He held out his hand. "Come with me."

Sophie took his hand and slid out of her bed. She stepped into the hallway and immediately noticed garland hanging over her doorway. "Oh, that's pretty." She walked down the hallway and entered her living room and kitchen space. She stopped and looked around.

On her front door there was a fresh, green wreath decorated with bright red poinsettias and red and gold ribbon. Her small kitchen table held a festive holly and ivy centerpiece with a tall red candle in the center. Her windows in the living room were lined with

141

stings of bright multi-colored lights that blinked in random patterns.

Each window held one white battery-powered candle. Hanging from

the light in her living room was a sprig of mistletoe. Her

entertainment center was strung with the same pine garland that was

hanging over her bedroom door. And in the corner of her living

room was a seven-foot tall white spruce tree. The tree was decked

with multi-colored lights and flashed randomly like the ones in the

windows. Ornaments of different colors and sizes hung on the

branches. A string of red metallic garland was strung around the tree

and it was topped with an angel in a bright red dress and dazzling

white wings. There was no tree skirt. Upon closer inspection Sophie

saw that the tree was in a planter so it could be planted outside once

spring arrived.

She stopped and looked over everything silently. Then she

looked over at Nick. His eyes were on her, waiting for her to say

something. "Nick, it's beautiful," she breathed. "I haven't had

Christmas decorations since college."

Nick smiled. "I know. I wanted to do something special for

you. Christmas is my favorite time of year and I want it to become yours as well. It's hard to get into the spirit when you don't deck your halls." He took her hand and led her to the center of the living room under the light. "Look up, my lady. I happen to be standing under the mistletoe."

Sophie grinned. "You'd better watch out. Some lady might just come and sweep you off your feet."

Nick pulled her into his arms. "I think she already has," he whispered.

Sophie looked up at him and he gently placed his lips on hers. "I love you, Sophie."

She sighed happily hearing his words. "I love you too, Nick." She had almost forgotten how nice it was to have your home decorated for the holidays. She also was pleased that Nick had given her a real tree that could be planted in the spring. She definitely planned to find a place in the park to plant the tree after the ground thawed.

Chapter 11

That evening Nick returned to the North Pole to check in with Kringle. Christmas was now less than two weeks away. He felt like he was definitely making progress with her. He still really wanted to tell her the entire truth but he knew he couldn't. Nick headed to the workshop to check in on the toy progress. He wanted to make sure that every good girl and boy would have a present.

The workshop was actually much larger than one would imagine. The complex was made up of several buildings, each one designed for the building of different types of toys. This one was a massive brick building with several floors that took care of fine details that somehow got missed during the creation process. One floor touched up electronic toys. Another painted dolls and action figures. Yet another shrink wrapped and packaged board games. Each elf had a different skill and was assigned to the area that best fit with his or her skill set. There were supervisors in each department and a manager for each floor. Kringle was the head of all of it.

Nick approached Kringle's office and knocked on the door.

"Come in!" Kringle's high pitched voice squeaked from inside. Nick opened the door and entered.

Kringle's office looked nothing like the office of a head of a company is expected to look. His office was painted various colors. One wall was bright lime green. Another was cerulean blue. A third was brick. And the wall with the door was camouflage. A hideous purple velvet sofa lined the bright lime green wall. Various photos of different elves in the building hung on the wall above the sofa. Across from the sofa against the cerulean blue wall was a large work table with various parts of toys on it. There seemed to be no organization to the parts at all. They were scattered across the table. Kringle's desk was near the brick wall. It was a long, L-shaped monstrosity made of various bits of metal welded together. There was a half dead plant on the corner of the desk. A plastic inbox sat on another corner overflowing with various papers of different colors. More parts of toys were piled in another section of the desk and a completely blank desk calendar in the center of the haphazard items on the desk.

Kringle looked up to see Nick entering. "Ah, hey boss. I know you're here to check in."

Nick nodded. "Yep. I want to see how we are progressing. Have you checked the number of toys against the nice list?"

"Absolutely! We seem to be right on schedule. If we continue making a couple of hundred toys a day between now and Christmas Eve we'll be just fine. And I have Fizzle checking the list twice right now to make sure we don't miss anyone." Kringle cracked his knuckles one by one. "Something tells me that checking on progress isn't your only reason for being here. What's on your mind?"

Nick sat down on the corner of the odd metallic desk. "Kringle, do you happen to have a copy of the prophecy in your desk?"

Kringle nodded. "Of course I do! Ha ha! What a silly question." He grabbed the overflowing inbox and began rifling through the papers. He grabbed one and held it up. "Found it! Now, why do you want it?"

Nick sighed. "Kringle, read it to me. I need to know word for word what it says."

Kringle cleared his throat and began to read:

A prophecy has been foretold

In a place that's always cold.

A wife for you eternally

If you follow what you see.

Kind and helpful, nice and sweet

Mrs. Claus will be a treat!

She'll love you with all her heart

And you will never be apart.

One week alone you'll have to find

The woman for which these years you've pined.

One week a year. If she's not found

Then home alone that year you are bound.

The Search for Mrs. Claus
To be the one she must be

Pure, chaste, and untouched.

Keep her pure until you say

The words "I do" that special day.

There are rules that you must follow.

I know that this is hard to swallow

But she absolutely cannot know

That you are he who has to go

Deliver toys on Christmas Eve

Else it destroys everything.

She must love you as a man alone

And with her heart her love is shown.

If she's the one that you adore

You'll ask the question with knee on the floor

On Christmas Eve for her to see

And then you'll tell her everything.

If she agrees and then says yes

You'll marry then with only two guests

To witness your eternal love

Be sealed forever with stars above.

She will then immortal be

And have some power that you can see.

Forever will she live her life

As Mrs. Claus, your perfect wife.

Nick listened carefully to each word and his heart sunk a bit. The prophecy was very clear in what must be done.

Kringle carefully watched Nick's face. "What? You've got something on your mind. Spit it out."

Nick looked down at the elf. "I wanted to tell her who I really am. I wanted to bring her here and show her what her future holds and then see if she will agree to marry me. It just seems like I am pulling the wool over her eyes, so to speak. She's thinking that I'm just an old man who works for a toy company. But she doesn't know that she's falling in love with a lie. She deserves to know the truth."

Kringle wagged his finger. "Naughty, naughty. That's something you absolutely cannot do." He hopped out of his chair and stood on his desk beside Nick. "Look, you love her. She loves you. This is going perfectly and according to plan. Just go with the flow." He patted Nick on the arm. "I know you want her to know the truth about you but if you do it messes up everything. And Christmas is less than two weeks away. You really don't want to spoil this and mess up your future."

Nick nodded. "I know. I just worry that once she knows the truth she'll say no. Then we'll have to start all over."

Kringle looked at Nick quizzically. "So you're saying you'd rather just settle with whoever wants to live forever than make absolutely certain you are with the right one?"

Nick paused. "No, that's not what I am saying at all."

Kringle held up his hand. "Wait. That is what you're saying. You're not trusting that the prophecy will work. If you don't follow it then you're pretty much guaranteed zero success. Sure, you might find a woman and marry her but if she isn't the one from the prophecy she won't become immortal like us. She'll grow old and die and you'll still be here. Do you want that? Or do you want a forever wife?"

"Obviously, I want a forever wife," Nick huffed. "What kind of a weird question is that?"

Kringle pointed his finger at Nick. "Then you follow the rules and do what it says and you'll get one. Capiche?"

Nick sighed reluctantly and nodded. "Fine. I may not want to do it this way, but I will. I'll follow the rules. Like you said, we have less than two weeks until Christmas. An answer to my question will come soon anyway."

Kringle hopped off his desk and settled back into his chair. "Good. Now get going. I've got more work to get done here."

Nick left Kringle's office and closed the door behind him. Sometimes that annoying elf got on his nerves but Kringle was right. As much as he didn't want to, Nick was going to have to follow the rules on this and trust that Sophie will be the one the prophecy was referring to when it was written.

Chapter 12

If there was one thing Sophie was it was determined. Ever since she left the hospital she'd been thinking about her conversation with Mira. Mira didn't believe her when she'd told her she thought Nick was Santa Claus. Sophie didn't care if Mira believed her or not. She believed it. She just didn't know how she was going to prove it.

Sophie remembered back to her childhood and thought of the song *Santa Claus is Coming to Town.* The part about going to find out if you've been naughty or nice stuck out in her mind. Santa legends foretold that the toys were made by elves and that the elves watched for children doing good and bad deeds and reported back to Santa. Never in her life had she seen an elf. If Nick was Santa, then she may see them coming to report to him one day. Even though this was a long shot, she decided to start watching for elves. After all, if she were able to see one delivering information to Nick in some way that would be all the proof she'd need.

Sophie had finished working and finished her performance on that cold windy night. There wasn't much time left until

Christmas Eve. If Nick really was Santa she wanted to prove it before then. As she walked home from her performance she thought of how Nick seemed to just disappear after they parted for the evening. She remembered how she'd heard him walk down the stairs but never saw him leave the building. As she walked along the snow-covered sidewalk she wondered if she could follow him without him knowing it and catch a glimpse of where he was going.

She reached her apartment building and headed inside. In the foyer area was just the door, a hallway to the first floor units, and the stairs up to the second floor where she lived. There was no other exit on that floor except a fire exit. If Nick had used the fire exit the alarm would have sounded. She climbed the stairs to the second floor and let herself inside her apartment.

As soon as she flipped the switch the Christmas lights came on as well. Nick had set up the decorations so beautifully. Her apartment was so festive and inviting now that he'd decorated. She almost hated to admit it, but the apartment felt much more like home now that it was decorated for Christmas.

Sophie paused and remembered back a few days ago when he'd done this for her. She remembered being sleepy and had laid down for a nap. When she awoke just a few minutes later her entire apartment was decorated. This much decorating should have taken at least half a day. How had he gotten it done in just a few minutes? She remembered looking at the clock and realizing that only a very small amount of time had passed.

A knock on her door interrupted her thoughts. "Who is it?" she called out, even though she knew it would be Nick.

"It's me," came Nick's reply muffled through the wooden door.

"Come on in honey," Sophie called out as she laid her coat over one of the kitchen chairs.

Nick opened the door and came in. He was carrying a pizza box. "I hope you don't mind but I brought dinner."

She smiled and walked over to him. "Awesome. I really wasn't planning on cooking tonight." She took the pizza and set it on the counter. Then she turned and slid her arms around Nick's neck and hugged him tightly. "I missed you today."

His arms tightened around her and he gently kissed her cheek. "I missed you too, my love. I'm so sorry I couldn't make it to the performance tonight. Things have been…a little hectic in my work schedule this week and I don't anticipate it letting up over the next couple of weeks either."

Sophie took in his words and mulled them over. "I assume because it's Christmas that toy production has increased."

He nodded and released her. "Definitely."

Sophie reached into the cabinets and brought out two plates and two glasses. "Nick, I've got a question for you. We've been dating for a couple of weeks now and I don't even know your last name. What is it?"

Nick froze. "You really won't believe me if I tell you so I won't say it right now."

Sophie turned to face him. "Why do you think I won't believe you?"

He smiled weakly. "Well, if I tell you my name you're going to think I'm some iconic figure instead of just being me, a man who loves you."

Sophie smiled at him. "Oh, come on honey. I just want to know. After all, if we ever take things further I'd like to know what my name could change to."

Nick smiled. "Then I'll tell you on Christmas Eve. Do you think you can hold off until then?"

Sophie shook her head. "I don't think so. I think I know your name but for some reason you're trying to keep this from me."

Nick looked into Sophie's eyes. He knew at that moment that she knew. Somehow, she knew who he really was. "And if I were who you seem to think I am, would that change how you feel about me?" He placed his hands on her shoulders. "I'm not confessing one way or the other, but if I am that iconic figure would you love me any more or less?"

Sophie shook her head. "No. I love you for you. I love Nick, the man standing in my kitchen who brought me pizza. It doesn't matter if you are San..."

Nick shushed her and placed a finger vertically against her lips. "Hush, don't say it. Whatever you do, don't say it. Just please...wait until Christmas Eve. You'll know more then. I can

157

assure you of that." He gathered her into his arms. "Sophie, just know that there are some things I want to tell you but I cannot until that night. Please, please just believe me and go along with this for now. A lot is at stake and I don't want to mess it up for either of us."

Sophie snuggled against him. She knew it. She'd hit the nail on the head. He was Santa Claus! But for some reason he couldn't tell her now. Why not? Why couldn't he tell her who he was? As much as she didn't want to wait, she knew she'd have to just wait until Christmas Eve. Apparently he was going to tell her all about it then.

She popped in a movie and they sat on the couch with pizza and cokes. Sophie didn't even really pay that much attention to the movie they were watching. She was far too busy thinking about Nick's alter ego. What did he look like in the Santa Claus costume? What was the North Pole like? Would the elves and the reindeer like her? So many questions ran through her mind.

After the movie Nick got up and carried their plates and glasses to the sink. "My love, it's late. I've got a lot to do tomorrow, so I need to call it a night."

Sophie got up and walked up to him in the kitchen. "Before you go, there's an event I'd like us to attend. The homeless shelter I work with is having a benefit banquet and ball on Friday night. It's a black tie affair so we'd have to really dress to the nines if you know what I mean. It's to raise money for the shelter and help keep it operating next year. I go every year but have never had a date for the event. Would you like to go with me?"

Nick smiled. "I'd love to. Friday's just a few days away and it would be fun to go to a dinner banquet and ball with you. What time should I pick you up?"

Sophie smiled. "How about seven? That gives us time to get there and have time to spare. It starts at eight."

Nick grinned. "Then it's a date!" He pulled her into his arms and kissed her deeply. "I'll see you on Friday then. I'll pick you up right at your door."

She nodded and grinned back. "I'll see you then!"

As Nick walked out the door she heard his footsteps going down the stairs. She stepped out of her apartment and slowly descended the stairs as well, staying far enough back so that he couldn't see her. As she peeked around the corner she saw a brilliant

flash of white light that blinded her and heard a faint pop that

sounded like a bubble. She rubbed her eyes and looked again. Nick

was gone.

Chapter 13

Friday arrived quickly. Sophie had arranged to be off that night so that she could attend the benefit banquet and ball. The affair was being held at a five star hotel across town. Earlier that year she'd bought a ball gown for this benefit banquet. It was an emerald green A-line dress that fit her perfectly. The bodice was lined with green rhinestones that glittered in the light. It was sleeveless but had an emerald green chiffon shawl that matched the flowing chiffon material of the lower half of the dress. She had a pair of shoes dyed to match.

Sophie put her hair up in an elegant bun and put on her mother's pair of emerald earrings and matching necklace. She looked and felt like a princess in this dress. She remembered when the hotel bought it last year and it was absolutely perfect. She wore it a couple of times a week. When Jeff offered to sell it to her at a reduced price after last year's Christmas season she jumped at the offer. Of all of her dresses this was her favorite. The color matched her eyes and it just made her look and feel elegant.

Shortly before seven she heard a knock at her door. "Come on in Nick," she called out.

The door opened and Nick walked in. He was so handsome! His beard and hair were combed and he was wearing an Armani tuxedo that must have been made especially for him. He looked so amazing! Sophie gasped and her mouth fell open. "Oh my! Nick, you look positively dashing! Every woman at this event is going to be all over you!"

He laughed heartily. "Well, they are welcome to try, but there's only one woman that will be allowed to be all over me." Sophie noticed that his laugh did in fact sound like the "ho ho ho" of Santa Claus.

She smiled. "Well, that's good to know. I'd hate to lose you to some other beautiful woman at the party." She walked over to him and gently kissed him. "Let's go."

She put on her heavy long, black coat and they headed outside. Sophie paused when she saw a long black limousine parked outside her door. "Wait a minute. Is this our ride?"

Nick opened one of the doors. "You are correct. After you, my lady." He helped Sophie into the limo and he climbed in after her." As soon as they were settled the smooth luxury vehicle pulled away from the curb.

Sophie has never been in a limo before. The seats were all black leather. "Wow, this is a beautiful car."

Nick smiled at her. "As they say in the movies, you ain't seen nothin' yet!" He pressed a button on the door and a flat screen television rose out of the wall by the driver. "You can even watch satellite TV in here." He pressed the button and it went back into the wall. "There's champagne and flutes for them. There are pretzels, peanuts, and other snacks. I rented it for the evening so you're welcome to anything you want."

"Wow, you really didn't have to do this, but thank you! I've never been in a limo before." Sophie ran her hand over the exquisite leather seat. "What a nice surprise!"

Nick pressed a button on the door and Christmas music began playing softly. The songs were traditional Christmas carols. "I know we both prefer these done traditionally so I picked out a CD

for the ride. I hope that's all right."

"You know it is, my dear," Sophie replied as she leaned back

into the seat. The sound of the Andrews sisters singing *We Three*

Kings filled the limo and Sophie began singing along. Nick

hesitantly joined in.

As the song ended Sophie turned to him. "I didn't know you

could sing! You have a wonderful voice!"

He blushed a bit. "It's not all that great, but I do enjoy

singing along when I know the words."

It wasn't long before the limo arrived at the hotel. A valet

opened the door for them and helped Sophie out the back seat of the

limo. The pair walked inside the hotel and they both checked their

coats in. Nick offered his arm to Sophie and she gladly accepted it.

The pair entered the ballroom.

This was an extremely large space with high ceilings that had

to be over twenty feet high. Gold chandeliers hung from the ceilings

bathing the floor in soft light. One side of the ballroom held tables

that were already set for the meal and place cards were on the plates.

Nick and Sophie wandered around the tabled until they found their place cards. They seated themselves and soon their table was filled with other smiling, happy benefactors here for the homeless shelter.

Nick and Sophie chatted politely with the others at their table. Dinner was soon served and it was exquisite. There was roasted duck, a variety of vegetables, dinner rolls, salad, and dessert was vanilla bean cheesecake. Wine was included in the meal so everyone at the table had a couple of glasses with their dinner.

After the plates were cleared a string quintet entered and began playing a waltz. People began to leave their tables and head to the dance floor to dance with the quintet's music. Nick turned to Sophie. "Tell me, do you dance?"

She nodded. "A little. I took lessons when I was a child, but it's been a really long time."

Nick took her hand and stood up. He led her to the dance floor and pulled her into his arms. "Just follow me." He began to waltz and Sophie waltzed along with him. She fumbled a little but he was so graceful on the dance floor that she really had no trouble following him. She moved along as he led the dance. She felt like she was floating! She'd danced before, but it never made her feel like this.

The waltz ended and everyone politely clapped. The musicians began playing again and Nick and Sophie began dancing once more. Sophie was amazed at how well Nick danced. He glided smoothly over the dance floor and carried her along effortlessly.

After that dance ended Sophie and Nick left the dance floor and walked hand in hand around the room chatting with others. The musicians were playing, people were chatting, and the homeless shelter was raising money for operating costs for another year. Nick stepped away to get another couple of glasses of wine for them.

Sophie watched him move across the room. He looked so incredibly handsome in that tux! As he approached the bar she saw an older woman walk over to him. Sophie's eyes narrowed as the woman put her hand on Nick's arm. She could see the woman laughing. Clearly this woman was flirting with Nick. Jealousy was not something that Sophie had ever experienced before. She watched as the woman was obviously trying to charm Nick. Nick smiled politely at the woman, picked up the two wine glasses, and retreated back to Sophie without even giving the other lady the time of day. As Nick reached her Sophie looked back at the woman. The woman's eyes widened as she saw Nick give Sophie a glass of the wine and slide his arm around Sophie's waist. Sophie met the woman's eyes with a glare. The other woman looked away and disappeared into the crowd.

Nick watched as Sophie's eyes were on the retreating woman across the room. "What was that about?"

Sophie turned back to Nick. "Boy was she flirting with you while you were getting the wine!"

Nick nodded. "That she was. She was telling be about being newly single and how she'd like to show me her helipad sometime." He winked at Sophie. "She was nowhere near as interesting as you are, my dear. Besides, I don't have a helicopter so I don't need a helipad."

Sophie breathed a sigh of relief. "Well, that's good to know. See, I told you other women would be all over you. You're quite the catch."

He laughed heartily. "Well my dear I am glad you think so." He took a sip of his wine.

She sipped hers as well. "I had no idea you were such an incredible dancer! Where did you learn to dance like that?"

He winked. "Back in my day, learning to dance was required of gentlemen. So few people can dance properly in this day. It seems like 'dancing' now is just twisting your body into weird, uncoordinated movements. There's no skill involved in that. You just move."

"That's definitely true. I can't do any sort of modern dance. I'm far too introverted and uncoordinated for that." Sophie sighed. "It is what it is."

"Well, I like the fact that you can ballroom dance. You're pretty good yourself." Nick asked.

"It wasn't something that I stuck with but learned the basics." Sophie looked out on the dance floor. The band was just beginning to play and the people on the dance floor began to foxtrot.

Nick held out his hand. "Can you foxtrot?"

Sophie nodded. "A little. I am sure I don't foxtrot nearly as well as you."

"Well, let's find out." Nick grabbed her hand and led her onto the dance floor. They began dancing together once again, gliding gracefully over the dance floor.

The song ended and people politely clapped once again. A man stood up with a microphone and began speaking. Everyone left the dance floor and went back to their seats. The man announced how much money had been raised for the homeless shelter that evening and what an honor it was to be able to help such a noble cause.

As the evening ended Sophie and Nick left the ballroom and retrieved their coats from the coat check. He helped Sophie into her coat and put his on. They left the hotel and the limo was waiting for them. The valet opened the door and Sophie and Nick climbed inside.

"This was a wonderful evening Nick. Thank you for coming with me." She leaned over and gently kissed him.

Nick's arms wrapped around her and he pulled her against him. He could smell her perfume and it made his heartbeat quicken. Softly he nibbled her neck. "Sophie. Oh my darling Sophie." His voice was soft but hurried. Desire crept into him as his lips traced down her neck. Her groan of delight made him pull her tighter against him.

"Nick..." His name escaped her lips quietly. "I want you..."

Nick's pulse raced. "Oh my love, I want you too." His voice was heavy with desire.

Sophie pulled back and looked into his eyes. They were dark with desire and hers were the same. "Then stay with me tonight."

Nick couldn't speak. He wanted to stay with her so much. However he knew what would happen if he did. He thought about the prophecy and about Kringle's words. He knew that even though they both wanted to he couldn't do it. "Oh my love, I want to so badly but I can't. You know it and so do I."

She sighed, frustration evident in her tone. "I know...but it doesn't make saying no easy. We both want this. We want it very much."

He nodded. "I know, my love. Someday soon we won't have to say no any longer. But until then…" He leaned down and kissed her forehead. "Until then, we have to stay pure."

"How much longer? Is this one of those things you'll tell me about on Christmas Eve?" Sophie's voice was quiet and she snuggled against him.

"Yep, it is. Just be patient until then and you'll know everything." Nick's voice was soft as he held her against him.

Nick knew Kringle was watching and had seen this exchange. He knew that Kringle would give him a hard time about coming close to that line again. He wanted to stay with her more than anything else! But he knew he had to behave just a little while longer.

The limo arrived at Sophie's apartment. She turned to Nick. "Thank you for this absolutely wonderful evening. I had a wonderful time with you."

He smiled and hugged her tightly. "I did as well, my love. Shall I walk you up?"

Sophie nodded. "That would be nice."

The pair exited the limo and entered Sophie's building. Slowly they ascended the stairs in silence. The desire was still hovering in the air and Sophie still had hopes that Nick would change his mind and stay for the night.

They stopped at her door. Sophie faced Nick and spoke, her voice soft. "You could sleep on the couch if you wanted to."

Nick sighed. "Honey, we both know that wouldn't happen. Believe me, I want to stay more than anything. But I can't. Not just yet." He gathered her into his arms and kissed her deeply. She melted against him, groaning as his tongue warred with hers.

Nick broke the kiss gently and stepped back. "What are your plans this weekend?"

Sophie took a moment to catch her breath. "Mira invited us to a Christmas party she's hosting at a bar. It's on Saturday night. I wasn't sure if you'd be interested in going or not."

Nick nodded. "It's not my usual hangout but if you're going I'll go. Honestly, I just want to be wherever you are."

She smiled. "Well I'll be there. It's at McMurphy's on the south side of town."

"Ah, I've heard of it. What time is the party? I can meet you there if you like." Nick's fingers traced slowly over hers as he held her hands in his.

"It's at nine. Mira likes to party late." Sophie laughed gently. "She's a bit of a wild child."

Nick grinned. "I've noticed. I'll meet you there." He leaned in to gently kiss her once more. "Goodnight, love of my heart. I'll see you tomorrow."

Nick turned to head back down the steps and Sophie entered her apartment. She headed for the window and saw that the limo was gone. She didn't remember hearing it drive away but it must have after they'd gone inside. She remembered seeing Nick disappear in a bright flash of light and hurried back into the stairwell to see if she'd see him disappear again. However, tonight he exited the building. Slowly Sophie followed him.

Nick walked across the street and into the park. Sophie stayed far enough behind as to not attract attention and kept her eyes on him. After a while Nick stopped walking. Sophie ducked behind a nearby tree but continued to watch him.

173

She saw another bright flash of light. This time it was bright purple. She also heard that familiar pop. She expected to see Nick gone. Instead she saw a tiny old man standing in front of Nick. This little old man was very thin. He had a long, dark gray beard that hung to the middle of his chest. He wore a bright pink top hat with a flamboyant neon pink feather in it. His clothes were red and he wore striped red and white socks. The hat absolutely did not go with his outfit at all!

Then it dawned on Sophie. This must be an elf! She strained to listen to their conversation very carefully.

"You were really getting close to that line again, Nick! I thought I might have to cause a car wreck in front of you to get you two to stop fawning all over each other!" The elf's voice was high, squeaky, and clearly angry.

"Kringle, I didn't cross any lines. She's still a virgin and so am I. The prophecy isn't broken." Nick's voice was exasperated as he spoke to Kringle.

"Well, technically you're right, but you sure do like coming close to the line. Why do you keep putting yourself in this predicament? If it wouldn't destroy the prophecy I'd go along as a chaperone every time you two went out. You most definitely need one! Keep your hormones to yourself until you marry her!" Kringle yelled.

Nick sighed. "I did, I did. You know she asked me to spend the night. Oh I really wanted to! I'd love to go back to her place and stay with her. But I'm behaving. For the sake of the prophecy I am behaving."

Kringle nodded. "Good. Come on. Let's get back to the North Pole. You need a snow shower!" Kringle disappeared in a flash of purple light and a popping sound. Nick followed suit, disappearing in a flash of white light.

Sophie wrapped her coat tightly around her and began walking back to her apartment. She'd finally done it! She'd seen an elf! And she definitely knew that Nick was Santa Claus. But what was this prophecy that Kringle mentioned? She really wanted to know what it was. Apparently this was what was preventing Nick from telling her what he wanted to tell her and it also prevented Nick from taking her to bed.

She headed back into her apartment replaying what she'd just seen in her mind. So, whoever this Kringle elf was must be someone of great importance to Nick and to the North Pole. Kringle must be the keeper of this prophecy, whatever it was. She hoped Christmas Eve would arrive sooner. Now that she knew a bit about what was happening with Nick behind the scenes she wanted to know the rest of the story.

Chapter 14

Nick spent Saturday morning up in his office at the North Pole. He was checking his list twice just to make sure there were no naughty children on it. Floy Farr, one of the office elves arrived with another sack of letters to Santa and dropped the overflowing mailbag on Nick's oversized desk. "You need a bigger inbox for these," squeaked Floy as he heaved the sack into Nick's plastic inbox.

"Maybe next year I can ask myself for one for Christmas," Nick joked as Floy left the room.

He poured through the last minute letters. Even though he had thousands of elves working he wanted to handle the mail himself. After all, these children had addressed the letters to him and he wanted to personally read each and every one of them. He picked up a red envelope, opened it, and began to read Bobby's request for a Lionel toy train.

Several hours later the stack of mail had disappeared and Nick had jotted down notes about the different wishes for each of the children. He checked the clock and saw that he had plenty of time before he had to leave for Mira's party. He really wasn't into the bar scene but he'd go for Sophie.

He looked at his calendar as he thought of Sophie. Christmas was a little over a week away now. He knew he'd have to find a ring for her. He tapped the water in a scrying bowl that sat on his desk and instantly saw the face of Kringle. The old elf was sitting in his office trying to put together a handful of spare parts. "Hey, come see me when you get a minute."

Instantly Kringle appeared in Nick's office. "Hey boss! What's up today? How's the mail?"

"Oh it's busy as usual this time of year. I don't get very many letters at all during the year but between November and December the post office is working overtime just to keep up." Nick handed Kringle the list. "Here are some additions to the nice list and their requests. I know it's late but can you please see if you can accommodate any of these? If you can't get them exactly what they wanted find something close. I want every good girl and boy to have something nice on Christmas morning."

Kringle took the list, folded it, and tucked it in his pocket. "Sure thing. I'll get it done."

Nick looked over at the elf. "Hey, I've got another question. We have eight days left until Christmas. I need to get a ring for Sophie. But I need advice. I've never bought a ring for a woman before. I want to find something she'll love and be proud to wear forever."

Kringle nodded and sat down in a chair. "Got it." The elf deepened his voice and spoke in a heavy British accent. "You need to find a ring that will not overwhelm the lady but accentuate her beauty."

"Something like that," Nick replied. "The price is no concern of mine. I'll make it happen. I just want her to have something beautiful and something that she'll love."

Kringle went back to his regular squeaky voice. "Look, just go to any jewelry store and see what they've got. If you don't like what you see, go to a different one. There are thousands of jewelry stores out there. Pick a country, find a store, and go from there."

Nick nodded. "I suppose I can do that. Well, since she's from Quebec I'll start there. I am sure there are plenty of nice jewelry stores that will have a lovely ring for my lovely lady."

Kringle grinned. "I bet they will! Go for it."

Nick popped on down to Quebec and found a jewelry store on the edge of the downtown area in an older brick building. He went in and began browsing the display cases. A friendly young woman approached him. "Hello and welcome! Can I help you find something?" She had a bright smile and wore diamond earrings. Her suit was charcoal and her long blonde hair was pulled back in a barrette. Her make up was perfect and she definitely looked the part of a classy jewelry sales woman.

Nick smiled at the young lady. "I am looking for the perfect ring for the woman I'd like to propose to on Christmas Eve. Can you show me what you have for engagement rings?"

The woman's eyes lit up. "Oh, certainly sir! Come with me. We've got plenty of engagement rings in stock. Can you tell me a bit about the lady so we can try to match a ring to her?"

Nick smiled as he followed the woman. "My lady is beautiful. She's kind and friendly. Her eyes are bright green and he has a beautiful smile that lights up the room when she smiles. Her voice is that of an angel and she can sing like Julie Andrews. She's sexy without trying to be and that's pretty amazing."

The woman grinned as they approached a display case filled with rings. "Tell me about the jewelry she currently wears. Is she into gold or does she prefer silver?"

Nick thought about it. "Honestly, I haven't seen her wear a lot of jewelry. Usually though it's more of a gold tone. She's a performer and gold lights up well on stage."

"Ah, gold it is then." The sales woman reached into the display case and brought out a tray with several gold engagement rings. The rings ranged from small stones to very large ones. There were so many different cuts for the diamonds. Nick wasn't sure where to turn.

"These are such different shapes. I had no idea that rings could come in so many different styles." Nick was beginning to feel a bit overwhelmed.

The sales woman nodded. "Oh yes, you can get a diamond cut into nearly any shape you want. Most engagement rings are round or princess cut."

"What's princess cut?" Nick asked.

"It's square, like this one." The sales woman pointed to a square, small diamond in a gold band.

"Ah, I see. I'm not sure I like that one." Nick pointed to a diamond that was larger. It looked like a cross between an oval and a diamond shape. It had to pointy ends and the sides were curved like an oval. "What's this shape?"

"Oh, this is the marquise cut. It's classy and elegant and will be perfect for any occasion." Her eyes were bright. "The many facets of the marquise cut make it sparkle whenever the light touches it." She pulled a small flashlight out of her pocket and shone it on the diamond in question. It lit up brilliantly. "What do you think about it?"

Nick smiled. "I really like it. It's gorgeous. Do you think my Sophie will like it?"

The sales woman grinned. "I haven't ever met a woman who didn't like a marquise cut diamond. They're absolutely beautiful."

An hour later after mulling over various rings in the store Nick walked out several thousand dollars poorer with the beautiful marquise cut diamond ring in a gold setting. He placed the ring box in his pocket, put his hands in his pockets, and closed his hand around the box as he walked down the streets of Quebec. His wanderings led him to the park across from Sophie's apartment. He stood just inside the park and looked up at her balcony covered with snow. The festive multi-colored Christmas lights shone inside her apartment so he knew she was home. He really wanted to walk up there and pop the question now. But he knew that to fulfill the prophecy he had to wait until Christmas Eve to ask her. He closed his eyes and popped back to the North Pole.

Nick headed to his bedroom and pulled the ring out of his pocket. He placed it on his nightstand right beside his clock and his lamp. He smiled as he looked at it. It wouldn't be long until he could ask her the question that burned within his soul. Will she say yes? He hoped that she would.

Nick disappeared and reappeared right outside Sophie's door. He knocked and heard her cheery voice call to him from inside. "Come on in."

He entered and Sophie was in her bedroom trying to decide on what to wear that evening. He walked down the hall and popped his head into her room. "Hey honey, I'm home," he said and smiled at her.

"Great! Then maybe you can tell me which sweater looks best with these pants. Should I go with the blue one or the red one?" Sophie held up two sweaters that had a very similar pattern.

"Well, I'm partial to red so go with the red one," Nick replied. "I love red. It's my favorite color."

Sophie smiled. "I bet it is. Red it is then." She picked up the red sweater and headed for the bathroom. He heard her voice call to him through the door. "I thought you were just going to meet me there."

He replied, "Well it's more fun to take you there and bring you home so I thought I'd come here. I hope you don't mind."

"I never do," came her reply through the door.

Nick went back out to her living room. The bright Christmas lights really made a difference in the ambiance. He sat down on the couch and a few minutes later Sophie came out of the bathroom. She'd pulled her hair back into a loose ponytail that Nick found incredibly sexy. She was wearing the bright red sweater with a long gold necklace that glittered against the red. She wore a pair of black slacks and black penny loafers. On her ears she wore small gold hoop earrings. She'd put on just a touch of make up to give definition to her eyes and a hint of lip gloss. Nick had to fight the urge to nibble that gloss right off her lips. He cleared his throat. "You look ravishing…and I do mean that literally, my love."

Sophie grinned. "I'm glad you approve. You look handsome as always! Are you ready?"

He nodded and stood up. "That I am. Let's go."

It was dark outside as the pair exited the building. Nick flagged down a cab and they climbed in and headed to McMurphy's Pub. The ride to the pub was quiet for them, but their cab driver was a talkative one. He kept talking about his favorite hockey team, the weather, the traffic, and anything else that happened to cross his mind. The driver didn't seem to mind that they weren't responding, as he was happy to talk about anything and everything.

The cab pulled up to the pub and the pair exited. Nick tipped the driver and wished him a Merry Christmas. "Merry Christmas to you pal," the driver replied and pulled away.

The sounds coming from the pub were noisy, raucous, and happy. Loud laughter and revelry could be heard even from the street. "Are you ready?" Sophie asked Nick.

"As ready as I'll ever be," he replied and took her hand. "Let's go party with Mira."

The pair entered the smoky pub. Pool tables were on the left side as you walked in the door. A couple of guys throwing darts were off to the right. The walls were dark brown wood paneling. Neon signs advertising various beers hung on the walls. The bar was on the left side past the pool tables. Several patrons of the bar were sitting on bar stools, drinking and carousing. It was clear that some had already had too much to drink. A karaoke DJ was setting up in the back of the bar. Sophie and Nick moved through the people until they saw Mira at a table near the back of the bar close to the karaoke area. She had several people with her. Sophie knew a few from work but most of the people she didn't recognize.

Mira had bleached her short, spiky hair a platinum blonde. She'd done it with gel so the spikes would stay up throughout the night. She wore a short-sleeved, faded blue t-shirt that advertised some sort of European beer. Her black jeans were tight and she wore a white belt with them. The t-shirt was a bit short so her midriff was showing highlighting her sparkling belly button ring.

"Hey Sophie! Nick! Over here!" Mira saw them and waved them over. She held a margarita in her hand. "Do you want a drink?"

Sophie nodded. "I'll take a Sprite please. I've got to work early in the morning so I don't want to get sloshed."

Nick nodded. "I'll also take a Sprite."

Mira called out to a waitress a couple of tables away. "Hey, bring my buddies here a couple of Sprites."

The karaoke DJ grabbed his microphone and began to speak. "All right ladies and gentlemen, thanks for coming out to McMurphy's Pub on this cold wintery night! It's time for some karaoke! Just fill out the little slip of paper with your name and the song you want to sing and we'll get you in the lineup. The specialty

tonight is Christmas music so come hit me up with some Christmas

songs!"

Mira turned to Sophie. "Sing something!"

Sophie looked at her half drunk friend. "You really want me

to?"

"Absolutely! You've got an awesome voice! No one here can

beat you!" Mira grinned and gave Sophie a gentle shove. "Go pick a

song."

Sophie approached the DJ and picked up a songbook. She

flipped through until she found something she wanted to sing. She

filled out the slip of paper and handed it back to the DJ and returned

to her table. "He'll get me in the lineup."

The waitress returned with their Sprites as the first singer

took the microphone and belted out a rather awful rendition of

Rudolph the Red Nosed Reindeer. Sophie rolled her eyes. She leaned

close to Nick and spoke loudly so he could hear her. "This is why I

typically don't do karaoke. People aren't very good most of the

time."

Nick nodded. "I know. You won't catch me up there singing."

Sophie looked at him. "But you have a really good voice. You'd do an awesome job."

He shook his head. "Honey, I really don't like to sing in public. I'll leave that up to you." He winked at her. "Besides, you're a lot prettier to look at."

She laughed as another singer took the stage. This lady had a decent voice and didn't destroy the song, for which Sophie was grateful.

The DJ then called Sophie's name. "That's my cue," she said to Nick as she got up and headed for the stage. She took the microphone and the words to *All I Want for Christmas is You* flashed on the TV screen. The moment Sophie began singing the bar fell silent. Her powerful voice carried over everyone as she sang. Even though she was in public, she kept her eyes locked on Nick. She was singing this song just for him. As the song ended everyone cheered and clapped loudly but she paid them no attention. She just looked at

Nick. She handed the DJ the microphone and headed back to her chair.

"I hope you know that's the truth. All I want for Christmas is you, my love." Sophie leaned over and softly kissed him. "I am hoping you'll be able to make my Christmas wish come true."

Nick's heart leaped in his chest. He slid an arm around her, leaned close, and spoke in her hear so only she could hear. "Well, I'll have to ask Santa if he can do that for you."

She giggled and looked up at him, her love showing in her bright green eyes. "I hope he can."

Mira grinned and applauded as her friend sat back down. "That's the ticket Sophie! Do another one!"

Sophie shook her head. "No, not tonight. I did one just because you asked me to. I'm good."

Mira rolled her eyes. "Oh, come on!"

"Why don't you do one, party girl?" Sophie asked her friend.

"But I can't sing worth a flip!" Mira exclaimed as she downed a shot of rum. "You're really a much better singer."

Sophie sighed and glanced at Nick. He leaned over and whispered in her ear, "You know I love your singing. Go for it."

She sighed and turned to face her inebriated friend. "Fine, Mira. I'll do one last one for you. But that's it!" Sophie flipped back through the book and found another song to sing. She walked back up to the DJ and handed him the little slip of paper.

Another rather horrible singer got up there. This man took the *Twelve Days of Christmas* and made up his own words to it. The words were rather funny but he was terribly off key.

Sophie turned to Nick and took a sip of her Sprite. "I know this isn't exactly the evening you wanted but thanks for coming with me. Mira just likes to party a little too much sometimes."

Nick nodded. "Oh, that's all right. Thankfully we don't have to worry about her driving home. She'll take a cab but will probably have one heck of a hangover in the morning." He watched as Mira put away another shot of rum.

The DJ called Sophie's name once more. "Here I go, again," she sighed. Sophie got up and headed for the stage. She took the microphone and the music began playing.

Sophie's clear, pure voice rang out in the smoke-filled bar as she began singing *What Child is This* for the half drunken crowd. As she sang many of the bar's patrons began listening and stopped drinking while she performed.

Nick watched her as she sang. If there was one thing that Sophie was extremely talented in it was drawing a crowd. Sophie had never considered herself beautiful but in reality she was gorgeous. The attention the crowd gave her Nick knew was not just for her beauty though. Her voice drew them in and they stayed for her appearance as well.

As the song ended Sophie handed the microphone back to the DJ. Once more the crowd erupted in cheers and applause. She smiled and bowed for the crowd. Even if they were half drunk she wanted to give a good performance for them. She stepped off the stage and walked back to Nick.

He was sitting in his chair just beaming as he watched her. "Sophie, you have the most exquisite voice I've ever heard. I know you love to cook but you really could have made it in the world as a professional singer full time. You've got the talent."

She smiled. "Thanks honey. I do, but I'm not really into the concerts and the drunkenness and revelry that tends to come with a musician's stardom. I prefer what I do. I like my little lounge singing and I love being able to cook at the hotel. I know it's not a glamorous job but it makes me happy."

Nick pulled her into his arms and softly kissed her lips. "Being happy is the main thing. I want you to be happy. I only hope that someday I'll be the one to make you happy as well."

Sophie snuggled close to him and kissed him back, her lips moving deftly over his. "You most definitely do make me happy, Nick. Even in the middle of a smoky bar as long as I am with you, I will be happy."

He held her tightly in his arms. He knew that as long as she was with him, he was happy as well. He loved her with all of his heart. Her caring and selflessness was a great asset and he wanted very much to be the man to make her happy. He only hoped that when he proposed to her that she would accept. He wanted to be there with her when she awoke in the morning and wanted to be the last thing she saw when she went to bed at night. Nick never knew love before, but now that he did he wanted to experience all of it. His

love was growing stronger by the day and he knew it would last

forever for her.

Chapter 15

Christmas was only four days away. The hotel was busier than ever and Sophie was seeing less and less of Nick. He said that it was due to business and she knew that was partially true. If he truly was Santa Claus then he'd be completely busy until Christmas had come and gone. But if he was Santa, would he still be around after Christmas Eve? Or would he just disappear back to the North Pole, never to be seen by her again? She hoped that wouldn't be the case.

Sophie's shift ended around six that evening at work. Nick had already told her he wouldn't be able to see her that night but didn't elaborate on why. She decided to go down to the homeless shelter and see if she could get a rough count of how many children were there this year. She really wanted to make sure she had enough toys for all of the kids.

The homeless shelter was on the other side of the park. It was a two story old brick building with a large kitchen and dining area. All of the rooms in the shelter were filled with beds and cots. Most of the beds and cots were occupied. She went inside from room to room greeting the people and counting all of the children she could

see. After her count was complete she was satisfied that each child

there did have a toy in her spare bedroom.

Sophie left the shelter and began walking down the street.

The wind was blowing bitterly cold that night and the falling snow

was quickly whipping into a blizzard. She pulled her coat tighter

around her and used her scarf to partially cover her face as she

walked. As she passed by an alley she heard a small bark. Sophie

turned her head to see a woman and a dog huddled in the alley.

She stopped and turned to the woman. She was an older

woman with short, curly white hair. Her face was weathered from

the years of hard living. Her bony hands had no gloves to cover

them. She wore a tattered, dirty brown jacket and had on a thin scarf

around her neck. She sat on the cold asphalt next to a dumpster. In

her lap shivered a Jack Russell terrier that she'd bundled inside her

old coat. Sophie approached the old woman. "Ma'am, there's a

shelter down the road. We really should get you out of this cold."

Her heart ached for this poor woman who was willing to stay out in

the freezing cold rather than leave her poor little dog out here all by himself. She knew the poor dog wouldn't make it through the night if left by himself in this blizzard.

The woman shook her head. "I've already been there, but they turned me out. Said I can't bring in Jack here and I'm not leaving him outside. The poor boy can't handle the cold and I'm all he's got."

Sophie looked at the little bundle of dog curled up in the woman's lap. He shivered in the cold and snuggled close to the thin old woman for warmth.

Sophie nodded. "I totally understand." She paused and looked around. "Do me a favor. Wait right here and I'll be back in about fifteen minutes, okay?"

The old woman nodded. "Jack and I aren't going anywhere. This is the warmest spot we've found so far." She settled back against the dumpster and pulled her old coat tight around her and the little dog.

Sophie stepped out of the alley and hurried back down the street. She stepped into the homeless shelter and pulled out her phone. After a search for low cost hotels in the area she found one with rooms available that did accept pets. She quickly booked a

room for one night. Sophie then hurried down the street to a nearby

pet store. She walked inside and found a small dog sweater and some

dog booties. She paid for the merchandise and called one of the

hotels nearby. After speaking to the chef there she rushed over and

he met her with a carryout bag of food.

Sophie hurried back down the street to the alley. The little

old woman and her dog were still there. "Hey, I'm back. I've got

something for your dog." She reached into the bag and pulled out the

sweater and dog booties. The old woman's face lit up and Sophie

helped her get the sweater and booties on her little dog. "Oh sweetie,

thank you so much for this!"

Sophie smiled. "Come with me. I've got a place for you to

stay for the night. And Jack's welcome there too." The woman's

mouth fell open in surprise, but she got up and followed Sophie

while carrying her little dog. The pair walked together down the

street in the blistering cold until they came to the hotel. They entered

and Sophie walked up to the counter.

The little man at the counter nodded as she approached. "Can I help you?" he asked.

Sophie nodded. "Yes, I am Sophia Laurent. I called earlier to reserve a room for the night."

"Ah yes, I remember you. You were looking for a place that accepts pets. Yes, we do allow cats and small dogs." The man spoke in a hurried voice.

Sophie nodded. "It's a Jack Russell terrier. He's very small."

The man handed her a key and Sophie paid in cash for the room. "You must be checked out by eleven. Continental breakfast begins at six and ends at ten. If you need anything else, just call. You're in room fifty-four."

Sophie thanked the man and led the woman down the hallway to room fifty-four. She unlocked the door and they walked in. The room was clean, warm, and had a television. There was a small bathroom with towels, soaps, and shampoo. The woman turned to Sophie and smiled with tears in her eyes. "Oh, thank you for this," she exclaimed with tears rolling down her cheeks.

Sophie handed her the bag. "This is some food from another hotel. I'm a friend of the chef there. I know it's not much but I hope this at least will get you and Jack out of the cold and give you food and a warm place for the night."

The old woman took the bag and set Jack on the floor. "I don't know how to thank you for this!"

"You don't have to." Sophie reached into her pocket and handed the woman twenty dollars. "This is all the cash I have left on me. Take it. It will help you out tomorrow."

"You are an angel, young lady. God bless you," the woman said softly before bursting into tears.

With a smile Sophie left the room so the woman and her dog could eat, bathe, and get a good night's rest.

Sophie headed out of the hotel and back through the park toward her apartment feeling happy. She'd felt so bad about the little old woman and her dog and couldn't leave them to freeze in this blizzard. She hurried through the park and into her apartment building. It was getting late and the wind was really picking up. She opened the door of her building grateful to be out of the freezing wind herself.

Kringle smiled as he watched Sophie enter her building. He tapped the water in the scrying bowl and the image of Sophie faded away. He disappeared with a pop and reappeared in Nick's office.

Nick was hard at work. Christmas was just a few days away and last minute preparations were in full swing. Hey boss, I hate to interrupt you but I wanted to let you know what I just saw."

Nick looked up from his stack of mail. "What's that?"

Kringle hopped up on the desk, knocking the stack of mail over. It tumbled into the floor in an untidy heap. "Oops. Sorry. Anyway, Sophie's proving herself to truly be kind, helpful, and friendly. She just took this homeless lady in off the street, bought her dog something to keep him warm, and rented her a hotel room for the night."

"She's really something special," Nick said gently. "She's an amazing woman."

Kringle looked over at him. "Hey, did you ever buy a ring?"

Nick nodded. "Yep, it's in the ring box on my nightstand. In just a couple of nights I'm going to find out if she'll marry me." Nick looked over at Kringle. "I hope this doesn't mess up the prophecy, but I think she knows the truth."

"How?" Kringle's eyes widened. "How could she know?"

"She asked me what my last name was one night." Nick spoke softly.

Kringle gasped. "And did you tell her?"

Nick shook his head. "No, I evaded the question. I did tell her that I'd tell her on Christmas Eve. She started to tell me that she thought she already knew what my last name was, but I interrupted her. Just in case she's not allowed to guess, you know. I don't want to mess this up."

"I know you don't. Three days. That's all that's left until Christmas. So technically you only have two days before you will be popping the question. Have you figured out where you're going to do it at?"

Nick nodded. "Yes, on the rooftop of her apartment building. During the day on Christmas Eve I'll be going with her to the homeless shelter to deliver the toys. Then that night I'm going to ask her to meet me on the roof at seven. I plan to have you and Mira there as witnesses. I'll tell her everything and then ask her. If she says yes, you get to perform a wedding. If she says no, I guess we disappear and she and Mira think this was some sort of crazy dream."

Kringle shrugged. "I guess that's what happens. The prophecy doesn't really specify what will happen in that case."

"Honestly I don't want to find out what happens in that case. I want her to say yes, marry me, and come back here to spend forever with me." Nick looked at Kringle. "You've been watching her too. Do you think she'll say yes?"

Kringle grinned and nodded enthusiastically. "I really do. She's crazy about you, she loves helping people, and she's got a heart of gold. Besides, who wouldn't want to live forever with Santa Claus? Yep, I really do believe she'll say yes."

Nick smiled. "I really hope so. I really do."

Chapter 16

Finally the morning of Christmas Eve arrived. Sophie woke up early, just as she always did. She had an early shift at work so that she could deliver the presents to the kids at the shelter in the afternoon. She dressed quickly and headed off to work.

Work on Christmas Eve was usually pretty quiet. No one was having Christmas parties or work events on that day. The hotel was desolate as well. Most people were with their families or home for Christmas. Sophie spent most of her day prepping for the next day's breakfast and was able to head home around noon. She changed out of her work clothes and put on a red Christmas sweater with a picture of Santa and a Christmas tree, her old comfy jeans, tennis shoes, and a heavy jacket. Even though she hadn't been able to contact Nick she knew he'd be there soon. They'd discussed this earlier and he arrived a half-hour later with a moving van full of toys. They carried the toys from Sophie's spare bedroom down to the van and loaded them up.

"Now, before we get going I need to change too." Nick

grinned as he headed to Sophie's bathroom with a duffel bag in his

hand. He came out ten minutes later in the full Santa Claus costume.

He had the boots, the pants, the coat, and the hat. He truly looked

like Santa!

Sophie grinned. "Oh, the kids are going to love this! You

truly do look the part."

Nick winked at her, his cheeks rosy. "That I do. It's

Christmas Eve so let's go brighten the day of some deserving kids."

The pair climbed into the van and Nick drove up to the

homeless shelter. The children were anticipating Sophie's arrival,

but they had no idea she was bringing a guest with her. When Santa

climbed out of the van the children squealed in delight. "Merry

Christmas!" Nick shouted loudly! "Ho ho ho!"

Inside the shelter a large recliner had been dragged into the

dining area. Workers unloaded the toys and placed them in a large

pile behind the chair. Nick and Sophie entered the building and Nick

headed for the chair. Sophie lined up all of the children and one by

one they came to see Nick. As she listened Nick called each child by name and asked them what they wanted for Christmas. After listening to them he reached into the pile of toys and pulled out a present, gave it to the child, and sent them on their merry way.

There were hundreds of children and it took several hours to get through the line. Through it all Nick was patient, kind, and friendly to each and every child and their parents. Sophie beamed as she watched him interact with all of the children and give them presents. This was what brought joy to her life. This is what Sophie worked for all year long. She wanted to be able to give back, to help these unfortunate children find a bit of happiness in the Christmas season. Watching them sit on Santa's lap and then tear into their present was amazing! This year having Nick play the part of Santa Claus was even better.

Nick was incredible! Sophie didn't know how he did it, but when each child sat on his lap he knew that child's name and age. He also seemed to know what they liked and what their interests were. She marveled as he asked Kevin about planes and how he asked Janice if her doll needed a new dress. Even the older children were into this. Sophie noticed how Marcus wanted an iPod and Nick pulled one out of his bag pre-loaded with songs that Marcus loved. Somehow Nick must have done his research and learned about these children before hand. Or maybe he really was Santa!

After all of the toys have been given out Nick and Sophie slipped out of the shelter. They climbed back into the van and Nick began driving back to Sophie's apartment.

Sophie turned to Nick and spoke gently. "That was the most amazing experience! Seeing those children's faces light up when you gave them their toys was absolutely the highlight of my year. I love doing this. I tell you, this was the best year of all. The kids really enjoyed seeing Santa Claus."

Nick laughed heartily. "I enjoyed giving them their gifts. These poor kids don't have enough happiness in the world, so it's good to give back. You've done a wonderful job for them for these past years."

She smiled. "Oh, Nick…by the way, it's Christmas Eve. You told me that you'd tell me your last name today.

He grinned. "That I did. I'll tell you tonight. Meet me on the roof of your building at exactly seven and bring Mira. She will need to be there too."

He stopped the van at her building. "Do me one other favor, my love. Wear the same outfit that you wore on the day we met. I love how the red looks on you." He leaned over and gently kissed her. "Will you be there?"

She smiled. "I wouldn't miss it for all the tea in China. Seven on the rooftop. Got it." She climbed out of the van and he drove away.

Sophie hurried back inside. Seven was about an hour away. She dialed Mira's number and Mira answered right away. "Hey, Sophie! Merry Christmas Eve!"

"Thanks, and the same to you. Look, I need a favor. Can you get over here right away? Nick wants me to meet him on the roof at seven and he asked that you come too."

Sophie could hear Mira's excitement through the phone. "Do you think he's going to propose?"

"Probably. I can't think of any other reason why he'd ask me to bring you along." Sophie spoke softly.

"Hey! Be nice," Mira chided.

"Sorry, but he's dating me and not you. Other than proposing I have no idea why he'd ask me to make sure you come. So can you come over?" Sophie's voice was pleading a bit.

Mira spoke quickly. "Yeah, let me grab my coat and I'll be there in a half hour. See you then!"

Sophie hung up the phone and headed into the bathroom to grab a quick shower. Tonight was Christmas Eve, a night of magic and mystery, and a night when people's dreams came true. She hoped that her own dreams and wishes would come true this evening as well.

When Sophie got out of the shower she dried her hair and dressed in the black pants and red shirt she was wearing on the day she met Nick in the park. She put on the same red hat and white scarf and donned her red wool coat.

Her doorbell rang and Mira walked in before Sophie could say a word. "Hey, what's up?" Mira asked.

"Nothing at the moment," Sophie replied. "It's getting close to seven."

Mira walked over to the balcony and looked up out the window. "Why in the world does he want to meet you on the roof? That's a little odd."

Sophie shrugged. "I have no idea. But I do know one thing. I've been asking him several questions now for some time. Mira, I still think he's Santa Claus. I bet that tonight he's going to confess to that being his real identity."

Mira turned back to Sophie. "Are you really still going on about that? Look at me and repeat…there's no such thing as Santa Claus."

Sophie laughed lightly. "I don't believe that Mira. I've seen an elf talking to him. Look, I know this sounds crazy, but I swear…I believe he's Santa Claus."

Mira looked at the clock. "Well, I guess we'll find out in a few minutes."

Sophie glanced at the clock. It read six fifty-seven. "It's close enough. Let's head up and see what he's got planned."

Courtney Daisey

The ladies exited Sophie's apartment and climbed the stairs

once more to the roof. Sophie placed her hand on the door handle

and looked back at Mira over her shoulder. "Well, here we go." She

turned the handle and opened the door.

The women stepped out on the roof and closed the door

behind them. The rooftop was bathed in a low glowing light. Sophie

and Mira both heard the sound of jingle bells. They stepped around

the corner of the stairwell entrance and beheld an amazing sight!

A large wooden sleigh was on top of the roof. It was made of

polished oak. The seat was covered in dark green velvet. The rungs

of the sleigh were carved intricately with images of holly and bells.

Standing in front of the sleigh were nine reindeer with impressive

antlers. The lead reindeer sported a brightly glowing red nose. The

harnesses on each reindeer were covered in silver bells that tinkled

and jingled brightly each time the reindeer shook or moved.

Standing beside the sleigh was a short, elderly elf that Sophie

recognized as Kringle, the elf that was talking to Nick that evening

in the park. He was wearing a bright green jacket and wore a brown

belt with a bright gold buckle. His shoes were dark green and he had a deep purple bowler hat on his head. His beard was dark gray and long and he wore a pair of gold-rimmed glasses.

Beside the elf stood Nick, only he wasn't Nick at all. He wore a red suit trimmed in white. A black belt was around his waist with a gold buckle. His boots were large and coal black. His head was covered in a red nightcap of sorts with a white tassel at the end. His eyes were bright, his nose and cheeks were pink, and his beard and hair were as white as the softly falling snow around them.

Sophie stood still and took in the sight. Mira's mouth fell open and she looked at Sophie unable to speak. Sophie turned to her friend and bluntly said, "I told you so."

Nick smiled and walked over to Sophie. "Sophie, I promised you that I'd tell you everything on Christmas Eve. Tonight is that night. Yes, you are correct. I am Nicholas Claus, otherwise known as Santa. This is my chief elf, Kringle." He motioned to the elf. Kringle bowed and smiled at Sophie.

Sophie smiled. "Hello Kringle. I've seen you once before though."

Kringle's eyes widened. "You have? Where?"

"In the park. I saw Nick talking to you one evening." Sophie watched as the elf blinked rapidly.

"Well…I'll have to be more careful. We're not supposed to be seen, you know." Kringle wrung his hands and looked down at the ground.

"Well don't worry about it. Mira didn't believe me when I told her that I thought Nick was Santa Claus." Sophie looked over at Mira. "Do you believe me now?"

Mira could only nod in agreement as her mouth dropped open in utter surprise.

Nick smiled and held his hand out. Sophie placed her hand in his. "Sophie, many years ago before you were born I became Santa. I once was a mortal man, but I was given the gift of immortality and the ability to make children all over the world happy. After I became Santa I was told of a prophecy. This prophecy stated that I would take one week out of the year to visit one city. I'd be looking for a woman who would be kind, helpful, friendly, and would be a perfect partner for me. I've looked for this partner for many years and you're the first I've found who fits the description. Part of the prophecy was that both she and I would be pure and untouched, which is true. That's why I had to fight the urge to be with you so hard. I didn't want to mess this up."

Nick dropped to one knee. "Sophie, I have no doubt in my heart that you are in fact the woman the prophecy referred to when it was written. I love you with all my heart and want to spend the rest of my days with you. I want to marry you and I want you to become Mrs. Claus."

Sophie's mouth fell open but Nick held up his hand. "Wait, please. Before you give me your answer, please hear me out." Sophie closed her mouth and Nick continued. "I can't give you eternal youth. I can't promise you money or luxurious things. But what I can offer you is my undying love and devotion. I can offer you immortality and a bit of Christmas magic, but you will age. You'll go from being thirty-five to sixty instantly once we're married. But you'll have peace in knowing that you'll live forever. I promise being sixty isn't bad at all. Part of the perks of being immortal is that you'll have plenty of energy!" His eyes twinkled and he winked at her. "Also, as immortals we will not be able to have children. However, Santa's children are all of the children in the world who believe."

Nick reached into his pocket and pulled out a small black box. "Sophie, now you know the truth. You loved me when you thought I was just a regular businessman. Will you love me now that you know I'm Santa Claus? I fell in love with you the minute we shook hands that day in the park. I can't imagine my future without you. Will you marry me and become my wife?"

Sophie's heart leaped in her chest. Not only was she right, but he was offering her marriage and immortality! Her voice was steady as she spoke. "Nick, I never thought I'd fall in love. I spent my life concentrating on my careers instead of guys. But the minute you took my hand I knew something was different about you. I knew you were someone special. I fell in love with you at that moment too. Even if you weren't Santa Claus and offering me immortality I'd still love you and I'd still say yes. Yes Nick, I will gladly marry you and become your wife!" Tears of happiness fell down her cheeks as she spoke.

Nick opened the box and pulled out the solitaire ring in the gold band. He slid the ring on her finger and rose to his feet. "I love you, Sophie. I love you now and will love you for eternity." He gathered her in his arms.

Sophie melted against him with tears of happiness flowing down her cheeks. "I love you too, Nick. I have ever since we met, and I always shall."

The romantic moment was broken by Kringle's squeaky voice shouting, "Yahoo!" Nick and Sophie turned to see him turning back flips in the sleigh. "She said yes! She said yes!"

Mira applauded as well, happy tears falling from her eyes as well. "Oh, Sophie, congratulations!"

Nick released Sophie and turned to Mira. "Here's where you come in. I'm marrying her right now. You are a witness and Kringle will be performing the ceremony."

Kringle cleared his throat and hopped up on the sleigh. "You're right! Let's have a wedding!"

Nick and Sophie stepped up to the sleigh hand in hand. Mira stood behind the happy couple as the snow fell softly.

Kringle cleared his throat. "Nick and Sophie, you both have declared your love for one another and you have declared your intentions to marry. Please face one another and Nick, take Sophie's hands in yours."

Nick turned to face Sophie and took her hands in his.

Kringle smiled and continued. "Nick, do you have any vows you'd like to make to Sophie?"

"Yes, I do," Nick said. He looked into Sophie's eyes. "From the minute we met I fell in love with you. I promise to love you for all eternity, to care for and honor you, and to always treat you with love and respect. You will be my equal from this day forward and I will always be yours."

More tears of happiness escaped Sophie's eyes as she listened to Nick's words. Kringle nodded and asked, "Sophie, do you have any vows you'd like to make to Nick?"

She nodded. "Yes, I do have some. Nick, you've made me realize that there was more to life than my career. You've shown me what it's like to love someone and to be loved by someone. I never realized that anything was missing in my life until I met you. I love you and can't imagine spending forever with anyone else. I love you and I always will."

Kringle grinned. "Then, by the power vested in me as Chief Elf of the North Pole I now pronounce you husband and wife. Mr. Claus, you may kiss your Mrs. Claus!"

Nick smiled at her. "I love you and I always will." He gathered her into his arms and covered her mouth with his.

The instant their lips touched the air crackled as if filled with lightning. Bright lights erupted over the building and covered the couple. The light intensified until neither Mira nor Kringle could see Nick or Sophie. As the light slowly dissipated they could all see that Sophie had changed. Her dark hair was now snow white. Her clothes had changed into a red, velvet dress trimmed with white. It matched Nick's suit perfectly. She'd gained about thirty pounds and was pleasantly plump instead of slim and trim. Her eyes were still bright green and sparkled with delight.

She smiled at Nick and his eyes lit up. "My love, you are so beautiful! You were lovely young and you are beautiful now! Tell me, how does it feel knowing that you'll live forever?"

Sophie grinned. "It's liberating! People often ponder being able to live forever. Now I can! And the best part is that I get to spend forever with you!"

Nick laughed heartily. "My love, that's the best part yet!"

Sophie turned and looked at Mira. Her friend was crying happy tears. "Oh, Mira, can you believe this?"

Mira wiped her tears away. "Sophie, this is amazing! I am so happy for you!"

Sophie walked over to Mira and the two friends embraced. "Mira, there's one thing. I know you haven't had a place of your own for a while and have been living at home. Since I'm moving out, would you like my apartment?"

Slowly, Mira nodded. "If you don't mind, that would be fantastic! But how do I send your personal belongings to the North Pole?"

"Oh, don't worry about that. I'll ask some elves to come in tonight and remove the items you'd like to take to the North Pole," Nick replied.

Sophie released Mira and stepped back. "Promise you won't forget me."

Mira laughed. "How could I forget my best friend? You're going off to be Mrs. Claus! This is incredible!"

Nick walked over and pulled Mira into a big hug. "I'll take good care of her. I can promise you that." He released Mira and placed a finger on the tip of her nose. "Now, go into Sophie's apartment. You're tired. Fall asleep and have a Merry Christmas."

Mira instantly yawned. "Sophie, I'm going to get some sleep. We'll be in touch." She turned and headed back toward the stairwell.

Sophie watched as her best friend entered the building and closed the door. She turned to Nick, her expression forlorn. "She'll forget me, won't she?"

Nick nodded. "Yes. See, she didn't believe in Santa Claus until she saw me tonight. There's no faith in that." He sighed as Mira disappeared into the building. "She knows the truth but has faith in none of it. When she wakes up in the morning it will be as if you never existed in this world. Tonight will be just a dream for her. She'll think this apartment has been hers for years. There will be a new pastry chef at the hotel and a new singer for the lounge. She won't know your name. Neither will the people at the hotel or those you volunteered with at the homeless shelter."

Sophie looked into Nick's eyes. "But why?"

"It's to protect us. The only people who can see us or the elves are those that believe in us. Mira didn't believe until she saw me, the sleigh, and the reindeer. By morning she'll forget about you and it's best for us." He placed one finger lightly above Sophie's heart. "But your friendship will always live on in here. She may not remember you, but you will always remember her."

Sophie sighed. "I'll never see her again."

Nick nodded. "Not in person, but there is a way. I'll show you that once we get to the North Pole. But in the meantime, we've got some toys to deliver. I'll use that time to teach you about your Christmas magic. Yes, you have magic just like the elves and I do." Nick stepped into the sleigh and held his hand out to his wife. "So, Sophie with your eyes so bright won't you ride in my sleigh tonight?"

She grinned and took his hand. "I'd be delighted!" She stepped into the sleigh and sat down beside Nick.

Kringle hopped out of the sleigh and stood in the powdery snow. "Boss, I'll prepare for your arrival after your ride. See you then!" With a pop and a bright flash of pink light, this time, Kringle disappeared.

Nick picked up the reins and looked at Sophie with a twinkle in his eye. "My lady, this is what I love!" He looked at the reindeer. "Now Dasher, now Dancer, now Prancer and Vixen! On Comet, on Cupid, on Donner and Blitzen! And Rudolph too! Let's get this show on the road boys!" He shook the reins and each of the reindeer pulled with all their might. Slowly, the sleight moved forward. Then suddenly the reindeer took off at top speed. Sophie gasped as they approached the edge of the building. Then instantly they were climbing smoothly into the sky. She was really flying in Santa's sleigh!

Courtney Daisey

Chapter 17

The sleigh rose higher and higher. Sophie peered over the edge of the sleigh at the lights of Quebec growing smaller and smaller. As the sleigh reached maximum altitude Sophie realized they were above the clouds. The moon looked so large from high up in the sky. The bells jingled softly as the reindeer pulled the sleigh across the night sky. Sophie settled back against the velvet cushion enjoying the ride.

"Nick, I was thinking back to the story you told me of your past and how you were a carpenter with your father. Was that the truth? Now that I know you really are Santa, tell me the rest of the story. How did you become Santa Claus?" Sophie had to speak loudly so Nick could hear her over the sounds of the wind whipping past them.

Nick settled back into the sleigh. "All right. After all, I can tell you now without fear of reprise. Yes, every bit of it was true. I was born north of Paris. My father was a carpenter and he did built houses for a living. And I did learn how to make toys by whittling.

Throughout the year I'd make toys and on Christmas Eve the children would put their shoes outside. I'd leave toys in the shoes. When the children awoke on Christmas morning they'd find toys left for them. I began making more and more toys and it became a large affair."

"How did you get involved with the elves?" Sophie was fascinated as she listened.

"Well," Nick continued, "I accidentally met Kringle one year. He was a little old man, just as he is now. He appeared to me out of nowhere and offered to help me. He had no family and appeared to just be a wanderer. I took him in and he began helping me make these toys and also helped deliver them on Christmas Eve. After Christmas Eve was over he confessed that he'd been sent by a race of elves that lived up north. They were skilled craftsmen who needed an outlet for their creativity. Stories of my delivering toys somehow reached them and they decided they wanted to be a part of this and help me out. So they sent Kringle to me to find out if I'd be receptive to their help."

"Were you receptive at first?" Sophie asked.

"Oh, most definitely!" Nick replied. "Kringle offered me immortality if I came to the North Pole and partnered with the elves. I'd distribute their toys and they'd be able to use their talents. It was a win-win situation for everyone involved. Apparently, I was part one of the prophecy. You were part two."

He paused and took a deep breath. "Our operation began much like the image that television has portrayed Santa's workshop to be. There was a single building with a long wooden table and elves making toys by hand. Over the years things have become more sophisticated up there. You'll see it soon, I promise. I do hope you'll like it as much as I do."

They flew along in the dark night sky. Above them they saw only bright stars. The moon seemed so large that Sophie almost felt like she could reach out and touch it. She looked over at Nick and asked another question. "Tell me something. You've heard of *NORAD Tracks Santa*, right?"

Nick laughed. "Oh yes, I've heard of it."

"Well? Is it true? Can they really track you?" Sophie asked, her curiosity evident in her gentle voice.

"Absolutely!" Nick exclaimed as he guided the reindeer along. "Although it doesn't work quite like you think. The reality of it is all Kringle's fault."

"It is? I've got to hear this. How is this Kringle's fault?" Sophie cocked her head to one side as her curiosity piqued.

"Kringle wanted to find a way to keep track of me while I was on my annual late night flight. He designed an SPS, or Santa Positioning System, to keep track of where the sleigh was. He added this little device to my sleigh one evening. Well lo and behold the frequency he used happened to be that of the NORAD system. NORAD started out as a joke for the kids but now it really does track where I am. Of course NORAD's employees don't know it's real." Nick winked at her.

"Wow, so they really can tell where you are and where you've been?" she asked.

Nick nodded. "They definitely can. Honestly, it's a helpful tool and it keeps me on track. If I start to fall behind Kringle will let me know so I can speed things up a bit."

The wind whipped past them as the reindeer galloped through the sky, Rudolph's bright red nose lighting the way. Sophie turned to Nick and spoke loudly enough to be heard over the wind and the jingling bells. "Honey, tell me something else. How do reindeer fly? What's the trick to it?"

Nick grinned. "Soph, that's part of the Christmas magic! Oh, that reminds me. I did tell you that as an immortal and my wife you've been granted the same magic that the elves and I have. Nothing's going to be the same for you ever again, believe me." He motioned to the reindeer. "The reindeer fly because of a special food that the elves make. For seven days before Christmas the reindeer eat nothing but this special grain imbued with Christmas magic. It's the magic given to the grains that allows the reindeer to fly."

Sophie nodded, her eyes looking out over the reindeer. Their antlers glistened brightly in the moonlight and the bright red light of Rudolph's nose cast a red glow over everything. "And Rudolph? Why is his nose red? Is that part of Christmas magic too?"

Nick nodded. "Yes. When he was born he had a red nose, much like the cartoon about him says that he did. The other reindeer

229

didn't like the fact that he was different and picked on him a bit. But one extremely snowy and stormy Christmas Eve years ago that light was the only thing that shone through the snow. So he became the lead reindeer and guides us through the sky every Christmas Eve now. It doesn't always glow but on Christmas Eve it glows brightly. I guess maybe it's the special reindeer grain."

"That's pretty cool. How do the elves make this special reindeer grain?" Sophie was full of questions and Nick had no objections to her asking everything. Now he was free to share all he knew with her. No more secrets would be kept between them and they both liked knowing this.

"I'm not exactly sure. Kringle knows the recipe and I am sure he'll show you. It's a long process that takes place throughout the year. As it's always snowy and the ground is frozen at the North Pole we have a large greenhouse where fruits and vegetables are grown. The elves have a section of that greenhouse dedicated to the reindeer grain." Nick flicked the reins and the reindeer turned to the right. "We're nearing our first house now. Are you ready to see how this works?"

Sophie nodded eagerly. "Absolutely! But I have to ask something else. How do you have time to deliver toys to all of the children all over the world? Logically speaking, there are not enough hours in the night to delivery toys to all of the children. I've always wondered how this part works."

Nick grinned. "Simple! Magic yet again! I'll explain it after we deliver to the first house. Ready?"

She nodded and watched as the sleigh began its descent toward the homes below. Nick slowed the reindeer down as they passed over a neighborhood. He reached into his pocket and pulled out a device that looked like a remote control with several large buttons on it. He pressed the buttons in a pattern. The buttons lit up and the device beeped a few times. Then the sleigh began to speed up again and rose back into the air. "There. That neighborhood is delivered."

Sophie cocked her head to one side. "What? You didn't even slide down the chimney! How did you deliver the toys?"

Nick laughed heartily. "This is an ingenious device that Kringle invented. Like you said, there isn't enough time in the night to deliver toys to all of the children. Technically, we don't deliver to all children in the world, but I'll get to that later. Because of the numerous toys per child and the sheer number of children, this device actually makes the deliveries automated. Before Christmas Eve arrives the elves program this device with what toys in the magic sack behind me belong to which child. I just have to press the buttons and the toys automatically disappear from the bag and reappear arranged under a Christmas tree and in the child's stocking."

Sophie laughed. "Oh, so that's how it's done! I guess this is a good way to avoid security systems too."

Nick grinned. "Absolutely! It also lets me avoid being seen, although kids never stop peeking. They love to try and spot Santa."

"Wait!" Sophie exclaimed. "What about the milk and cookies? And carrots that some people leave for the reindeer? I can remember being a child and waking up on Christmas morning to find that glass of milk gone and bites taken out of cookies and carrots. Does this device do that too?"

Nick nodded enthusiastically. "That it does! It actually returns the milk to the gallon in the people's refrigerators and tears bits out of cookies, apples, carrots, or anything else the children leave out. The bites of food are deposited into people's flowerbeds or woods and the children think I've eaten them."

Sophie giggled. "That's pretty awesome! I guess that it would be impossible for Santa to eat a bite out of every cookie left on a plate for him."

Nick howled with laughter. "Santa's supposed to be chubby and plump, but I wouldn't be able to fit into this sleigh if I really did eat a bite out of each and every cookie left out for me! Oh, we're coming up on a small town. Let's deliver this one."

He slowed the sleigh down once again and pulled the device out of his pocket once more. "Would you like to do it this time?"

Sophie froze. "What if I press the wrong button?"

He smiled. "Oh that's impossible. The order of the buttons isn't important, nor is how many times they are pressed. You just have to press them near a town or house and it does the rest. Go on. Do it." He held the device out to her.

Slowly, Sophie took the device. There were five buttons on it in red, green, blue, purple, and pink. She hesitated for a moment and then pressed several buttons. The device lit up and beeped a couple of times. Then Nick sped the sleigh up again and it rose back high in the sky. "Congratulations! You just delivered your first Christmas presents!"

She grinned and handed the remote back to Nick. He pocketed it as the sleigh rose again.

"Wait a moment! Even with this device, you won't be able to really travel all over the entire planet fast enough to make these deliveries. How do you do that?" Sophie looked over at her husband quizzically.

"Magic yet again, my love!" Nick said excitedly. "One of my skills is the ability to manipulate time. I can't stop it completely, but I can slow it down immensely, or speed it up if I need to do so. Tell me something. Do you remember as a child that it seemed like Christmas Eve was the longest night of the year? Didn't it seem like it took forever for Christmas morning to arrive?"

Sophie nodded. "Yes, I can remember waking up in the middle of the night looking at the clock and thinking that hours had to have passed only to realize that it was a few minutes."

Nick winked at her. "It wasn't your imagination. It was me, manipulating time. I have to slow time down to a crawl in order to make this happen. It takes a lot of concentration every Christmas Eve to slow time down enough to make these deliveries happen. I admit, it does help that we don't really deliver presents to every child."

"Why not?" Sophie frowned. "Aren't all good little girls and boys supposed to get presents?"

Nick nodded. "Technically, yes. However, I can only go where I am welcome. There are some families who celebrate Christmas but don't believe in Santa. I can't go there because they don't believe in me. Also, there are cultures and groups of people who have never heard of Santa. I can't go there because they don't believe in me either. I can only go where people believe and want me to be there. Oh, and on the rare occasion that a child truly has been so naughty that they can't get a Christmas present, I can't go there either."

"Does that happen? Can a child really be so naughty that they can't get a Christmas present?" Sophie asked, her voice soft.

Nick nodded. "Yes, it can happen. It's very, very rare though. This year we only have a handful of children who are on the naughty list. Usually it's because of more bad behavior than good throughout the year. See, we try to give these children every chance of getting a gift. I hate for anyone to go without a present on Christmas. It's just unkind. But if their bad deeds outweigh their good ones, they get removed from the nice list and put on the naughty one. They can come off the naughty list with good deeds though."

Sophie nodded slowly. "Oh, I see. So are all of the children's deeds throughout the year weighed for this?"

"Yes," Nick replied. "We can't count one month or one week. After all, everyone has an off day sometimes. So giving all of their actions and deeds for the year fair weight generally ensures that the child will get a Christmas present. And typically the better behaved the child is, the more presents he or she will receive."

236

"Being good really does pay off," Sophie commented.

"Better believe it! I'll be making my list and checking it twice. I'll definitely know if you've been naughty or nice." Nick grinned at her.

"Oh, speaking of that, how do you know if the children have been naughty or nice? Do the elves really spy on kids to make sure they are behaving and then report back to you?" Sophie questioned.

"Something like that. As you know, the legends say that the elves are watching to see if children are being naughty or nice and then they report back to me. That's partly true. The elves are watching but are not always physically there. There's far too much chance of someone spotting them, as you spotted Kringle. He'll never live that down, believe me. It's a badge of honor for elves to not be seen. For those who are, the others give them a bit of a hard time. It's all in good fun of course, but they'll always be remembered at the elf who got spotted." Nick flicked the reins again and the sleigh flew lower. He pulled out the device, pressed the buttons, and guided the sleigh back into the sky again.

"Another neighborhood done. We're falling behind so we'd better speed up." He snapped the reins and the reindeer flew faster. "There we go. We'll be able to catch up now. Believe it or not, we're on a strict schedule on Christmas Eve. Now, where was I? Oh, yes. Elves watching children." Nick cleared his throat and continued. "Most of the time the elves use a scrying bowl. That's a large clay bowl filled with magic water."

"Water with Christmas magic in it?" Sophie asked.

"Well of course," Nick replied. "They can touch the water and think of the child they want to check on and the bowl will show them exactly what that child is doing at that moment. It's pretty amazing really. Then the elves can monitor their assigned children and update my naughty and nice list without even having to leave the North Pole. It also means that they have less chance of being spotted. They are required to go out and personally check on their children at least once a year. The daredevils like to go more often, but it's not required. I think they get a thrill out of the chance they might be caught."

Sophie giggled. "I can imagine they brag about their close

calls and how many times they've been out without being seen."

Nick grinned. "Right you are! They do like to brag about

that."

They flew along in silence for a while as Sophie took in all of

the information she had just learned. There was a lot of magic

involved in the whole Christmas thing. She listened as the sound of

the jingle bells sounded through the night as they flew and delivered

presents. "Honey? I've got another question for you."

"Fire away," Nick said as they hurried along through the sky.

"Well, I can remember a time as a child on Christmas Eve

when I know I heard your sleigh. I was at my grandmother's house

and didn't want to go to bed. My cousins and I were awake and

looking out the window and I know we heard your sleigh bells. All

of us heard them. We looked out the window and didn't see

anything, but we all know we heard you flying overheard. At that

point we all hurried off to bed because we didn't want you to pass us

by. So, can people really hear your sleigh?" Sophie looked over at

him as she awaited his reply.

Nick smiled happily at her. "Absolutely people can hear my sleigh. Once again though, only those who truly believe can hear the bells or catch a glimpse of this sleigh flying in the sky. Most people as they grow older stop believing and lose the ability to hear me coming or see me."

"So, is that how it works? People age and stop believing so they don't get presents any more?" Sophie's eyes were focused on the reindeer as they flew, but she listened intently to what Nick has to say.

"Well, sort of. Typically around the age of thirteen most children stop believing in me. Some stop sooner and some stop later. There is a very small handful that never stop believing but because they are adults I can't deliver presents to them. After all, we make toys and nothing else." Nick leaned back into the cushion of the sleigh as he spoke. "Those adults still have the ability to see me and hear my sleigh bells. Even though I can't give them presents they still believe in the magic of Christmas. But for those who stop believing in the magic, they stop believing in me. When that happens, for them I cease to exist. Fortunately, there are other children who are born and come along who will believe. It's a bit of job security. There will always be children who will believe in me. And it's for them that I do what I do."

Nick looked over at his wife. "That, my dear, is probably the most in depth explanation of Christmas magic that I've ever given. But there's more too. That magic lives in us."

"It does? You'll have to explain that to me." Sophie listened as Nick cleared his throat once more and began to speak.

"Well," he began, "you remember when we were going to go out and your hair was wet? Remember how suddenly it was dry? Well, that was me."

Sophie elbowed him lightly. "I knew it! I knew that was you!"

Nick nodded and grinned. "Yep, it was me. See, because the magic lives in us we can do some magic too, even more than manipulating time. I didn't want to risk you getting sick so I dried your hair with magic. We are able to do almost anything that is good. But, there's one thing we can't do. We can't save lives or bring people back from the dead." Nick sighed. "When you went under the water I was as helpless as the other bystanders. Even though I wanted to, I knew my magic couldn't save you. For that I need to turn to a greater power."

"You mean God?" Sophie asked.

Nick nodded. "Yes. Even Santa is saved and turns to God for help sometimes. I might be able to do a lot through the gift He has given me but there are still things I can't do. That's why while you were in the hospital I prayed. I wanted Him to save your life more than I've ever wanted anything else. And He answered my prayer."

Sophie reached out and covered Nick's hand with her own. "I'm glad He did. I wanted to be with you. You know I died that night for a short time. But I talked to my own father and he told me it wasn't my time. He also told me that he and my mother approved of you and to follow my heart. I'm so glad I listened to him!"

Nick smiled at her. "I am too. When you agreed to marry me I was the happiest man on the face of the earth. There's nothing I wanted more."

Sophie smiled at him. "Me too. I can't imagine a future without you in it."

242

Nick leaned over and softly kissed her. "Me too, my love. Now I really need to speed these reindeer up so we can get these deliveries made. Time to speed this up to my normal delivery speed." He cracked the reins and the reindeer sped off.

Courtney Daisey

Chapter 18

After what seemed like an eternity Sophie and Nick heard the remote beep and all of the lights lit up. "Well, that's that. All of the presents have been delivered," Nick yawned. "It's time to head home. Are you ready to see the North Pole?"

Sophie nodded excitedly. "Completely! I can't wait! I've been looking forward to this ever since you told me everything. What's it like?"

Nick slid his arms around her and pulled her close against his side. "It's unlike any place you've ever seen before. We're currently over Alaska now so it won't be long before we get home. I really hope you enjoy the North Pole. I know it's cold and barren but it's a wonderful, magical place and the elves and I are very happy to live there."

Sophie snuggled close to him. "I have no doubt that I'm going to love it too."

Nick flicked the reins. "Time to head home boys. You did a good job," he called to the reindeer. The reindeer all pricked their ears at his words and turned sharply to the right. They knew the way home and were heading north rapidly.

Sophie saw the northern lights as they crossed the Arctic Circle. The lights were various colors and snaked across the sky like brightly colored ribbons. She knew they weren't far at all from the North Pole. "How much farther is it?" she asked excitedly.

Nick grinned and pointed at a faint group of lights on the horizon. "See those lights there? That's our destination. That's my workshop at the North Pole. Are you ready to see your new home now?"

"Totally!" Sophie exclaimed. She clasped her hands together in anticipation of what she would find once they landed.

The sleigh and reindeer began a descent toward the lights. As they neared the North Pole Sophie could see numerous buildings with windows brightly lit. There was a smooth strip of ice and snow that was lined with elves holding candles. The reindeer began slowing down and the sleigh bumped slightly as they landed on that strip of ice and snow with elves lighting the place to land.

The reindeer trotted down the landing strip and stopped on the far side of it. The snow was covered with thousands of elves. Each one held a bright candle and watched as Nick stepped out of the sleigh. He turned and faced the large crowd and spoke, his booming voice echoing through the expanse around them. "Citizens of the North Pole, I have wonderful news! The prophecy has been fulfilled!" He turned and held a hand out to Sophie. "I'd like each and every one of you to meet Mrs. Claus! Her name is Sophie and I am so honored to have finally found the right woman for me. We married last night before the toy delivery and she'll now be residing here with us!"

The elves cheered. Kringle appeared with a pop on the seat of the sleigh. "Um, boss? I already told them about her. In fact, we've all got a present for Sophie." Kringle grinned at Sophie and held out his hand. "Come with me?"

Sophie smiled and placed her hand in Kringle's small one. "Sure!" She stood up and Kringle led her out of the sleigh. He led Sophie through the crowd of elves with Nick following behind them.

She noted that the elves were remarkably quiet. She supposed they were as curious about her as she was about them.

Kringle guided Sophie through the vast crowd of elves and away from the landing strip where the sleigh had stopped. She glanced back over her shoulder at the sleigh and saw nine elves each leading one of the reindeer away from the sleigh. "Where are they taking the reindeer?" she asked Kringle as they walked.

"To the stable. The reindeer have had an extremely long and exhausting night so they'll need a few days of rest." Kringle stopped at a large open space on the edge of the town. "Here we are!"

Kringle released Sophie's hand. The large open space was well decorated for a party. There was a stage with the set up for a band. Brightly colored lights were hung all around the stage and across the space as well. A large refreshment table was on the edge of the area. It was covered in a variety of cookies and cupcakes, finger sandwiches, and punch. There were glowing lights lining the edge of the vast area where the party was set up. Amazingly, the air was calm and Sophie wasn't the least bit cold.

She turned to the old elf and grinned. "So you guys have an after party, so to speak?"

Kringle giggled. "Something like that although it's not an after party celebrating Christmas. This is celebrating you. Sophie Claus, welcome to the North Pole! We've been waiting for you for a very long time and we are so excited that you are here now!" Kringle turned to face the elves. "Ladies and gentlemen, let's get this party started!"

Sophie clasped her hands together as several elves jumped up on the large stage and picked up various instruments. They began playing some rock and roll style Christmas songs. Kringle grabbed Sophie's hand. "Care to cut a rug, ma'am?"

She laughed happily. "Sure!" As Kringle led her out onto the icy dance floor Nick called after them, "Bring her back in one piece, Kringle!"

Even though their height difference was great, Kringle proved to be a fabulous dancer. Fast or slow, he could move. They boogied along to a hard rock version of *Carol Of The Bells* and applauded when it was over. Kringle led Sophie back to Nick and released her hand. "I've got more dancing to do. Be back later!" He scampered off back toward the crowd.

Nick slid his arm around his wife's waist. "This is how we party here at the North Pole. I hope you are enjoying yourself."

"Oh, I most certainly am! What a beautiful place!" Sophie turned and looked into Nick's eyes with a smile. "I wish I could have come sooner."

Nick leaned down and gently kissed her. "I do too. I even asked Kringle about it, but he said no. The prophecy was very clear that I wasn't supposed to tell you anything about my life here until you agreed to marry me on Christmas Eve." He sighed gently. "Believe me, I wanted to say something. I felt like I was being deceptive. I knew all about this and what your life would be like if you said yes and yet I wasn't allowed to say one word about it. The prophecy said that you had to love me as a man before you could be allowed to love me as Santa."

Sophie nodded. "I see, and I understand that. After all, what woman wouldn't give up everything for immortality and a life with you!" She winked at him. "You're quite the catch."

Nick laughed heartily. "Flattery will get you everywhere, Mrs. Claus!" He gathered her in his arms and held her tightly. "I love you so much!" He kissed her deeply.

Sophie melted against him as he kissed her. Her hands traced over the red velvet of the back of his Santa suit. Her heart leaped in her chest as she took in everything. She was here at the North Pole and had married Santa Claus! She would live forever and be able to continue helping children throughout the world by ensuring that they received toys. As the kiss broke tears of joy streamed down her face.

Nick reached up and wiped the tears away. "Is everything all right?"

Sophie nodded. "Absolutely! Everything is just perfect! I never expected that my life would turn out this way, but I am so happy that it did. I'm just happy and excited that it did!" She stepped back and took Nick's hand. "Shall we dance, honey?"

He grinned. "I thought you'd never ask!"

The pair stepped out on the dance floor just as the band began a slow song called *Where Are you Christmas*. Nick slipped his arms around Sophie and held her as they began dancing. Sophie looked around her as they swayed to the music. There were elf couples also dancing with the music. Other elves gathered around the refreshment table with little plates of snacks. More elves stood in small groups chatting with one another.

She realized that life at the North Pole wouldn't be lonely at all. She'd make new friends and would still be able to check in on Mira with one of those scrying bowls. She made a mental note to ask Kringle how to use one sometime.

As the song ended Nick stepped back and everyone applauded the band. Then suddenly Kringle was on stage. He took the microphone from the lead singer and began speaking. "Ladies and gentlemen, we've gathered tonight to honor and welcome Sophie Claus to her new home and to our lives." The elves hooted and hollered, cheering for Sophie.

She blushed brightly and waved at the excited crowd. People had never made such a fuss over her before. This was something totally new to her. She decided she rather liked this attention. One place she'd always received attention was when she was performing. Then she got an idea. She walked over to the stage and hopped up there beside Kringle. She held out her hand for the microphone. Kringle nodded and handed it to her.

Sophie cleared her throat and spoke to the crowd. "Ladies and gentlemen, thank you for being so kind and welcoming to me. I'm really looking forward to getting to know you all in the months to come. You do such wonderful things here for the children of the world and I can tell you that they greatly appreciate all that you do! I know that my husband is the guy who kind of gets all the credit, but children are always on the lookout for elves. You are definitely not overlooked nor forgotten. Elves are a large part of what happens here. I'm looking forward to learning where I'll fit in as well. Thank you for the warm welcome!"

The elves cheered as she turned back toward Kringle. "I know you want this microphone back now but there's something I have to do first." She turned to the band. "Can you play *Rockin' Around the Christmas Tree* please?"

The band struck a chord and jumped right into the song. Sophie raised the microphone and began singing in her powerful, beautiful voice. The elves danced and sang along as she performed the song. As the short song ended the elves cheered for her.

Sophie turned to the band once more and asked them to play one more song for her. They began a soft version of *O Holy Night* and Sophie's clear voice rang across the ice and snow as she sang. She hit the high notes beautifully and by the time the song had ended there wasn't a dry eye anywhere to be seen. The elves applauded her once more as she stepped off the stage and headed back to Nick's side.

Nick smiled at her as she took her place beside him. "I think they like your singing."

She nodded and looked out over the crowd. The band had begun performing again. Suddenly Sophie felt a tug on her dress. She looked down and there was a young elf there. "Mrs. Claus? I just wanted to tell you that you have a really pretty voice! Thanks for singing and I hope you do it again soon."

The elf was a young male. He had brown hair and no beard or glasses. He wore a bright yellow tunic, black pants, and black and white striped stockings. His shoes were bright yellow with a jingle bell on the end of the toe that curled back over the shoe. His hat was black with a bright yellow feather in it.

Sophie smiled and held out her hand to the elf. "Well thank you! I love to sing so I am sure I'll do it as often as I can. What's your name?"

"Twinkle, ma'am," he replied in his little voice. It was not as squeaky as Kringle's but was still higher than most humans.

She shook Twinkle's hand. "It's nice to meet you Twinkle. I look forward to getting to know you!"

Twinkle grinned and shook her hand vigorously. "Me too!" He turned and bounded back over to another group of young elves.

A moment later she felt another tug at her dress. She looked down and this time found herself looking into the dark brown eyes of a female elf. This elf woman appeared to be of Asian descent and had dark black hair and brown eyes. She wore a dress made of pink chiffon and had a pair of little pink high heels that perfectly matched her dress. Her long hair was twisted up into a bun and she wore a pink ice necklace and matching pink ice dangling earrings.

The elf woman spoke in a high feminine voice. "Hi and welcome to the North Pole, Mrs. Claus!" She held out her hand. "I'm Arlyss, one of the elves who makes costumes for children to play dress-up with! I love to sew and even made my own dress!"

"Well it's absolutely beautiful!" Sophie exclaimed as she shook Arlyss's hand. "I hope we become good friends."

"I do too," Arlyss smiled and releases Sophie's hand. "I'll see you later!" She walked off back toward the dance floor.

One by one more elves came up to introduce themselves to Sophie. She noted that the elves were very much like humans. They came in different sizes, colors, and nationalities. They seemed to have their own personalities and preferences. They all wore different clothes, which were very different from the image she had in her mind of everyone wearing red, green, or variations of Santa's suit.

Sophie turned to Nick. "I know I'm going to have a tough time remembering everyone's names and jobs they do here. You may have to remind me."

Nick laughed lightly. "Oh, you won't need any help with that. That's one of the perks of being immortal now. Immortals have incredible memories. Once you meet someone for the first time you'll have no trouble remember everything that they tell you about themselves."

"Really?" Sophie asked.

"Nick nodded. "Yep, really. For example, look over there." Nick motioned to an elf in a red velvet dress. "What's her name and what does she do?"

Without hesitation Sophie replied, "Her name's Marlene and she works in the wrapping and packaging department."

Nick grinned and motioned to another elf. "What about him? Who is he?"

"That's Bobble and he sweeps up after each shift is over." Sophie realized that Nick was right. "Wow! I really can remember everyone!"

Nick winked at her. "You bet you can! How else do you think Santa knows the names of every child in the world? That's why I make it a point to read my own mail. It helps me continue to know all of the children and remember what they like. Sometimes I take a chance and give them a present that I'm not sure if they will like or not, but I always try to make sure that every child gets something they're interested in each year."

Sophie nodded. "Ah, that explains something then. Back at the shelter you knew every child's name and what he or she wanted for Christmas. I wasn't sure if you'd just done your homework on the kids there or if you were the real deal."

Nick grinned. "Yep, I'm the real deal!" He turned to face Sophie. "Speaking of those kids in the shelter, that reminds me of something. I want to make sure they aren't forgotten in years going forward. Children in shelters and foster care have a hard enough time as it is and they deserve a good Christmas too. So I'm going to ask Kringle to reassign a handful of elves to monitor homeless shelters and foster children going forward and make sure we know where everyone is at Christmas. I don't want them going without a Christmas present any longer."

Sophie's eyes filled with tears at his words. "Oh, Nick, that would be wonderful! I was worried that the shelter kids might not get a good Christmas next year."

Nick shook his head. "Oh, no, honey. I wasn't going to let them be forgotten any longer. It's not going to be easy, but we can use the help of some talented elves to keep track of them."

"Thank you!" Sophie flung her around his neck and hugged him tightly. "I really appreciate this and I know they will to."

Nick sighed softly and hugged her tightly. She was right. The children in shelters and foster care had been forgotten far too long. But no longer will that be an issue. He knew Sophie would be more than happy to help him keep track of them so they could have a Christmas gift.

He released her and took her hand. "My love, I am getting a bit tired. Before we go to bed would you like a tour of the workshop and your new house?"

She nodded eagerly. "I'd love one!"

Courtney Daisey

Chapter 19

Nick led Sophie away from the large crowd and toward the center of the village that was their home. The buildings she saw were all made of red brick. Some had several stories while others just had one or two. Nick stopped beside one extremely large building. "This is the main workshop. Kringle's office is actually in here. There are smaller workshops as well but this is the main location for all of toy production." He opened the door and led her inside.

Inside the building looked like a typical office's reception area. There was a centralized desk, only it was small and perfectly elf-sized. It had no computer or phone on it though, but a large clay bowl sat in the center of the desk. The bowl was ornately decorated with red and gold paint and it was filled with golden colored water that shimmered in the light above it. There were various papers and inboxes on the desk as well.

"What's that?" Sophie asked as she pointed to the bowl.

"That's a scrying bowl," Nick replied.

"That reminds me, I need to ask Kringle how to use that," Sophie said softly.

"Oh, we can do that right now if you'd like." Nick smiled at her and called out to his chief elf. "Kringle? Are you around?"

With a pop and a flash of blue light Kringle appeared before Nick. "Yep, I'm here! What's up?"

Nick motioned to the bowl. "Sophie would like a lesson in how to use a scrying bowl. Can you teach her?"

Kringle nodded and hopped into the chair at the desk. "You bet I can!" He slid the chair up closer to the bowl and Sophie knelt down to watch.

"The bowl is filled with magic water. We never dump it out and it never gets dirty. The water is linked to all of the people in the world. The magic to use the bowl comes from within. For example, if you want to check in on someone you just lightly touch the top of the water and think of the person you want to check in with." Kringle looked at her. "Got it?"

Sophie nodded. "I think so."

"Oh, wait, one more thing! What you see in the bowl is only seen by you. If you are checking in on someone and another person walks into the room they can't see what you see. They'll only see the golden water. But if you want to share what you're seeing just hold that person's hand and they'll be able to see what you see in the bowl." Kringle held out his finger over the bowl. "Want to try it?"

Sophie nodded again. "Yes, I do."

Kringle touched the water. "I'm going to think of Bobble, who is still at the party. Let's check in on him." He reached out and took Sophie's hand and they both looked into the bowl.

The water shimmered and then the image of golden water changed. Sophie saw the ice, the lights, and Bobble dancing with one of the other elves on the dance floor near the stage. "Oh, wow," Sophie breathed. "That's amazing!"

"It definitely is!" Kringle agreed. "Now, to stop it just touch the water once more, like this." He touched the water and it shimmered once more before the image faded and Sophie saw nothing more than golden water in a bowl.

Sophie stood up and beamed down at Kringle. "That's one of the most amazing things I've ever seen in my life!"

"There are a few scrying bowls in Nick's house. Feel free to use them anytime! There's just one rule when using them. If the person is doing something private the bowl won't work. Nothing will happen when you touch the water. You won't be able to catch people having marital relations or using the bathroom, for example." Kringle giggled. "That would just be embarrassing!"

Sophie laughed. "Yep, that really would be. But that's good news. I'd hate to check in on my human friends and them be taking a shower or something."

Kringle nodded. "Definitely! So you don't have to worry about that."

Nick took Sophie's hand and they left the reception area. Kringle opted to follow them. He led Sophie through a door and into a large manufacturing plant. It looked like Lego's, Lincoln Logs, erector sets, and other building-type toys were manufactured here. She could see large vats of molten plastic of various colors. She saw little metallic discs on a machine that stamped them into gears and other parts.

"Wow, it's just like an assembly line," Sophie remarked as they walked through the plant. "It's much more organized than I pictured in my head."

"What had you pictured when you thought of the workshop? A wooden table with a bunch of elves sitting around it with hammers and lit by candlelight?" Kringle scoffed. "Thankfully, we're much more advanced now, though that is how it started." He grinned at her. "What do you think of it?"

"Honestly, it's really amazing! I never would have expected this to be what Santa's workshop was like." Sophie linked her fingers with Nick's as he led her through the tables and conveyor belts.

"See, down here they make the parts. Then the parts are loaded on the different conveyor belts. Upstairs are additional assembly points where specialists in these types of toys put them together in the right combinations for packaging. Once bagged in plastic bags they're sent further upstairs to the boxing room where

265

they're put in boxes. After all of that the complete toys are sent

through an underground conveyor system to the wrapping area.

There they are wrapped and tagged for delivery to some lucky little

girl or boy." Nick glanced at her as she listened carefully to his

words.

Sophie was quiet as she looked around at the fascinating,

modern system for building toys. "And you have different

workshops like this for every type of toy?"

Nick nodded. "That we do! If you think this place is

awesome you should see where we make electronic toys. The video

game system shop is really incredible! See, we actually have elves

who used their scrying bowls to tap into the creators of the various

game system and watched as the systems were built. They learned

how to recreate them to be identical to the systems created by the

true game system manufacturers. The children don't know that these

Xboxes or Playstations aren't made at Microsoft or Sony. It's pretty

ingenious really." They left the plant and walked back into the

reception area.

"So the elves that make those actually learned from the people who created the systems? Wow! That's pretty impressive." Sophie braced herself for a blast of cold air as Nick opened the door to let her outside. However, that blast of air never came.

The pair stepped out into the street with Kringle following them closely. They continued walking down the street. "Tell me something Nick. We're at the North Pole. Why can we walk down the street here without freezing to death? Yes, it's chilly, but I expected it to be much colder." Sophie could see her breath in the air a little, but she was expecting more of the cold.

Nick smiled at her. "My love, that's another part of the magic. Even though we're at the North Pole we have a bit of a shield around the workshop and my house. Well…our house now. This shield prevents us from being seen even if someone wanders right into the middle of town. The visitor just sees snow and ice. The visitors feel the cold though. It's bitterly cold and they feel it to their bones. We can see them in town. They are glowing bright yellow. We know that when we see a person glowing yellow we have to be absolutely silent. That glowing makes the person able to walk through buildings and he or she will never know he was here with us."

"Oh, really? So that explains why so many people have come on expeditions to the North Pole and haven't ever seen you or the workshop." Sophie was beginning to understand what an important part magic played in life here. There was so much she would have to learn.

"Absolutely! We've seen so many of these people exploring right through our town. But all the people see is a vast open icy space with blowing wind and snow." Nick winked at her. "For us, the shield keeps the cold and blowing wind out. We feel chilly, yes. But we aren't overwhelmed or frozen to death in it. You'll have no trouble walking around with just a light jacket here."

Sophie listened. More magic! She was beginning to think that there was nothing here that magic didn't touch in some way.

She knew that the North Pole was actually right in the middle of the Arctic Ocean. She couldn't remember exactly but thought that the ocean melted during the summer. She looked over at Nick. "Honey, I'm sorry I keep pestering you, but I have to ask this too."

Nick laughed. "Oh, you're not pestering me at all. I've been wanting to tell you all about my home. Now's your chance to ask me anything you want to know!"

"Oh, that's good!" Sophie motioned to the vast expanse of ice. "This whole workshop is on top of ice. What happens if the snow melts? Doesn't it melt during the summer?"

Nick nodded. "Most of it does. However, this shield that we live under helps keep our portion of the ice frozen. It will never melt. We live on the ice year round."

Sophie nodded. "Ah, I see. Well, that really does explain why you are so good at ice skating!"

Nick laughed. "You'll learn. One of these days with a little practice you'll be zipping down the ice just like the rest of us here. And you won't have to worry about the ice caving in either. The ice beneath us is about fifty feet thick so there's no chance that you will fall through."

Sophie smiled happily. "That's a relief!"

The night had been long but the sun hadn't risen. She knew from a science class in college that the North Pole was situated in a location where it was dark for a long time before the sun rose. A day here wasn't calculated by the movement of the earth and sun, but by hours alone.

Sophie yawned lightly. She'd been awake now for over twenty-four hours. Part of her was afraid that if she fell asleep she'd wake up and find that everything was just a very elaborate dream. She didn't want this to end.

Nick slid his arm around Sophie's waist. "Are you getting sleepy, my love?"

She nodded. "Yes. I've been awake for so long now."

"Well, why don't I give you a tour of our house? Then we can head to bed." He leaned close and placed his lips near her ear. "I hope you're not too tired yet."

Sophie grinned and whispered back to him. "Not at all. In fact, I'm really looking forward to that, my love."

Her words shot right into him and his pulse quickened. "Then we'll make this a shorter tour. Come with me." Nick led Sophie down the street toward an open square in the center of town. There was a large Christmas tree in the center of the square. It was decorate with brightly colored lights and ornaments. There was a large star on the top of the tree. Across the square behind the enormous Christmas tree stood a two-story log cabin home with brightly lit windows. The cabin was lined with multi-colored Christmas lights and candle lights in each window. A large evergreen wreath hung on the door donned with a bright red bow.

"Is that the house?" Sophie asked as they approached the square.

Nick nodded. "Yes, that's my home. Now it's your home as well, my love. I do hope you will like it."

"It's beautiful outside," she breathed. "I can't wait to see the inside!"

Nick and Sophie climbed the three stairs and stepped onto the house's porch. There was a large porch swing on one side. The other held a wooden table and four chairs with red cushions on them. Nick reached out and turned the doorknob. "Welcome home Sophie." Without warning he scooped Sophie up in his arms and carried her over the threshold.

Nick set his new wife down just inside the door. The walls were roughly hewn logs. They stood in a large foyer with a staircase that led to the second floor. There was a long hallway to the left and a door to the right. Wall sconces lit the open space. Sophie stood still looking at everything. "Nick! It's more amazing than I ever imagined! I love log cabins! This almost reminds me of a fishing trip I went on with my dad when I was a child. It's beautiful!"

Nick took her hand and led her into the room on the right. It was a large open office. Nick's wooden desk sat in the center of the room. Behind the desk was an enormous bookcase filled with many different books. The desk itself was made of white oak and was polished so that it shone brightly. The log walls were lit with more wall sconces and a dark green circular rug covered the floor. A tall floor lamp stood in the corner of the room adding additional lighting. The surface of the desk was completely clear except for one empty black plastic inbox and two wooden chairs sat in front of the desk. These chairs had green cushions that matched the rug on the floor beneath them. The chair that sat behind Nick's desk was a black leather high backed chair that looked elegant and yet comfortable.

"I love your office!" Sophie exclaimed. She stepped away from him and walked slowly around the room, taking everything in. She traced her fingers over the desk and the chairs. "This room suits you. And you're right. There's no computer or smart phone here." She laughed lightly. "So, I have to ask this. Where's your naughty and nice list?"

Nick grinned. "Actually it's with the elves. They monitor the list and send me memos with necessary updates. The list is so large now that we have to roll it up. It's more like a giant scroll than a list."

"You know, it amazes me that in a place that has really come into the modern age technologically that you don't utilize a computer to keep track of the list. It would be much easier, I promise." Sophie looked over her shoulder at Nick. "What do you say? Would you be willing to give it a shot?"

Nick sighed. "I don't know. I admit the elves have been asking me for the past ten years or so to start tracking the list on a computer instead of manually." He walked over to Sophie and took her hand in his. "Maybe I'd be willing to give it a shot."

She grinned at him happily. "That's great! I know it seems a bit daunting now, but the computer will be the best tool for business that you ever had! Now kids even like to send e-mails to Santa. I bet you could find a way to tap into those e-mails and actually read them."

"You make a very good point, honey. We'll see if we can get some elves to build me a computer soon." Nick led her out of his office and down the long hallway. He stopped at a room on the right. "This is the space that I think will most interest you."

He led her into the room and she gasped. It was a gourmet, professional kitchen. The appliances appeared to be brand new. They were stainless steel and shone brightly in the light. There was a large island in the center of the kitchen with an iron hanging rack with brand new, high quality pots and pans hanging from it. The sink was large and deep and made of polished copper. The cabinets hanging around the kitchen were a dark cherry and contrasted with the lighter color of the cedar logs that made up the walls of the log cabin. Across the kitchen was a large wooden table with handmade chairs.

She opened the drawers and they were stocked with utensils and flatware. "Oh Nick!" she gasped.

"Do you like it? Remember that time when I wasn't able to see you very often? It's because I was overseeing the remodeling of the kitchen up here. I had such hopes that you'd agree to marry me and I wanted to give you this as a wedding present." Nick watched her as she looked in every door and drawer in the kitchen. "I've got another small present for you as well." He reached into a cabinet and pulled out a red box with a bright green bow.

Sophie held out her hand and accepted the package. She opened it and grinned in delight. Inside was a bright red apron. She remembered that night when she made him dinner and was wearing the towels. "You remembered! I see I don't have to wear towels any longer in the kitchen. It's beautiful!"

Nick grinned back at her. "Do you like it?"

"I absolutely love it! How did you know? Wait, never mind. As Santa…you know." She smiled warmly at him. "How can I ever thank you enough?"

He smiled at her. "You already have. You married me."

She walked back over to him and slipped her hand into his. "I love this kitchen and can't wait to cook us a meal in here! Show me more!"

Nick led her out of the kitchen and into the room next door. It was a large living area. There was a tall Christmas tree in the corner decorated with bright multi-colored lights and plenty of ornaments. The tree was topped with an ornate angel and a Lionel train was merrily chugging along in a circular track around the tree. An oversized cushy green armchair sat in the corner and a matching green couch lined the wall across from the windows. There was a roaring fire in a red brick fireplace and the mantle was covered in green garland. A red and green wreath hung over the mantle. The floor was covered in a matching red and green rug. In the center of the rug was a large red scrying bowl. "This is the living room."

Sophie walked in and looked around. She smiled at the pretty Christmas tree and noted that it was a real tree. "Does this tree ever die?"

Nick shook his head. "No, this is an evergreen. Don't confuse our evergreens with the pines and such of North America.

This evergreen tree is planted in a pot, will never get any taller or wider, and is designed specifically for indoor life. It doesn't shed any needles either. As long as it's near a window where it gets light and we give it plenty of water it will live forever, just like us. I leave it decorated year round. After all, here at the North Pole it's Christmas every day of the year."

"Tell me something else, honey. I've noticed that you always use multi-colored lights. Why is that?" Sophie asked. "When I was a child we always used red or white lights."

"Well, honestly I think that multi-colored lights add character to the tree and the house. While elegant and pretty, plain white lights lack any personality. It's like a blank canvas begging to be painted. Sure they are lovely and classy, but I just really like the multi-colored ones. I don't intend to change that." He grinned at her. "I hope you don't mind them."

"Oh, no, I don't mind them one bit. They're pretty and they do give some personality to an otherwise blank space. I just wondered about that. I noticed when you decorated the tree you gave me it was also multi-colored. It seems like so many people are moving away from that and going to white or solid color lights now." She walked over to the fire and held her hands out to it. It was warm and cozy and the wood burning inside the fireplace crackled invitingly. "I do have one question. Where's your television?"

Nick shrugged. "I've never had one here. Do you want one? I am sure we can have one installed easily."

She nodded. "I rather enjoyed snuggling on the couch watching movies with you. We can definitely continue to do that but will need a TV to make that happen, unless you have a movie theater somewhere." She giggled.

Nick laughed. "No, it's a fairly large house but there's no movie theater."

Sophie eyed him. "So how come you're such a fan of movies when you don't even have a television in your house?"

Nick laughed. "During the week I'd spend looking for a lady like you I'd go to the movies from time to time. I fell in love with the silver screen. We'll talk with the elves tomorrow about a TV as well as the computer. Good grief, you're modernizing my house."

"Sometimes progress is a positive thing, my love," Sophie said gently. "A good movie and some pizza or popcorn will always make for an excellent date night!"

"Just a few rooms left in the house to see, honey." Nick took Sophie's hand and led her out of the living room and back down the hallway. They ascended the stairs listening to them creak comfortingly as they walked up. At the top of the stairs there was a short hallway to the left. Nick led her down the hallway and stopped at one of the rooms. The door was closed. "I've never used this room, but have been saving it for my wife. So this is for you."

He opened the door. Inside was a beautiful library. There was a smaller desk against the wall. Bookcases lined the walls and they were filled with books. The floor was covered in a burgundy rug. There was a comfy chocolate brown sofa against one wall. Another corner held a matching chocolate brown recliner. A wooden end table was next to the recliner and held a brass lamp.

Sophie walked in and looked around. Some of the shelves held photos and other personal items of hers. "Nick, where did you get these?"

"When Mira agreed to take your apartment I had some elves go in and remove anything that was personal of yours. All of those items are in here. There are photos, books, knick-knacks and other items that the elves saw as something important to you. So they brought them here. You can make this space whatever you want it to be. Even though we're married I still wanted to make sure that you had a special space of your own when you need time to yourself." Nick walked over to her and placed his hands on her shoulders. "I hope you like it."

She turned and looked into Nick's bright eyes. "I absolutely love it! You've made a wonderful space here. Don't think that you have to stay out of here. You are just as welcome here as I am."

They turned and walked out of the room. Nick led her to the next room and opened the door. It was a large, spacious bathroom. It was clear to Sophie that this room has been recently remodeled as well. The vanity was marble over dark cherry cabinets. New and shiny pendulum lights hung from the high ceiling. There was an extremely large shower enclosed in glass. The toilet was in its own room and was also brand new. And against the wall under the window was an oversized soaking tub made of porcelain. "Oh, my!"

Sophie exclaimed as she walked into the bathroom. "This is quite a

bathroom! It really dwarfs the one I had in my apartment!"

"Hey! I'm an elf, not a dwarf lady!" Kringle's squeaky voice

sounded from the doorway.

Sophie jumped when she heard his voice and whirled around.

"Oh! I completely forgot you were with us! Look, I was talking

about the size of my bathroom, not you!"

Kringle giggled. "I know! I'm just being…"

"Just being Kringle," Nick finished his friend's sentence.

"Only one room left to see, my love. That's the bedroom." An edge

sounded in his voice as he spoke the last word.

Sophie faced Nick and took his hand. "Honey, show me that

room please."

Nick led her out of the bathroom and to the bedroom next

door. Inside she saw a tall four-poster bed made of mahogany. The

comforter was red and plush throw pillows covered the bed. There

was a fireplace on the wall and a low fire burned in embers inside.

Each side of the bed had a nightstand with a lamp and an alarm clock on it. Nick's side also held a book, a nightcap, a clock, and a pair of reading glasses. There was a dresser against the wall under the window. On top of the dresser was a large dark red poinsettia.

Sophie walked into the room, her heart pounding. Here was his bedroom, which was now her bedroom. She looked at the bed knowing what would be taking place very soon. Her pulse raced and her breathing quickened. "I love it," she said softly. She turned and looked at Nick, her desire evident in her eyes.

The look in his eyes matched hers. He finally realized that they would never again have to deny their physical desires. "I'm glad," he whispered.

A high-pitched soft giggle was heard from the door way. Both Nick and Sophie turned at the same time and their eyes landed on Kringle who was snickering from the hall. "What?" he asked.

Nick walked over to the door and placed his hand on the doorknob. "Good night Kringle. Remember what I told you a while back. You can't be in my house tonight."

Kringle laughed a bit. "Oh, I remember that!"

Sophie smiled down at the elf and looked him straight in the eye. "Sleep well Kringle. Now please go."

Nick closed the door leaving Kringle standing in the hall alone. Kringle turned and began skipping down the short hallway singing his own rendition of *Silver Bells* as he skipped. "Silver balls....silver balls...it's Christmas time in the bedroom..."